"I want y

Jake's words stopped Siobhan in her tracks. How she longed to believe him! But her instincts told her to flee, as quickly as possible. Jake was dangerous. He had already torn her heart in two.

A shudder ran through her as she stood there. She was unable to move, wanting to run, but needing him too.

Jake gently lifted her in his arms and carried her into the bedroom, then lowered himself beside her on the bed. "Your skin smells so sweet," he groaned, burying his face between her breasts.

His caresses grew more intimate, and soon Siobhan was gasping with pleasure. "I've...I've never felt this way before!" she breathed. Then her hands began to touch him, want him, feel him, and all her reasons for running away were forgotten....

Dear Reader,

We at Harlequin are extremely proud to introduce
our new series, **HARLEQUIN TEMPTATION**.
Romance publishing today is exciting, expanding
and innovative. We have responded to the ever-
changing demands of you, the reader, by creating
this new, more sensuous series. Between the covers
of each **HARLEQUIN TEMPTATION** you will find
an irresistible story to stimulate your imagination
and warm your heart.

Styles in romance change, and these highly
sensuous stories may not be to every reader's taste.
But Harlequin continues its commitment to
satisfy all your romance-reading needs with
books of the highest quality. Our sincerest wish is
that **HARLEQUIN TEMPTATION** will bring you
many hours of pleasurable reading.

THE EDITORS

U.S.
HARLEQUIN TEMPTATION
2504 WEST SOUTHERN AVE.
TEMPE, ARIZONA
85282

CAN.
HARLEQUIN TEMPTATION
P.O. BOX 2800
POSTAL STATION "A"
WILLOWDALE, ONTARIO
M2N 5T5

Chameleon

DANIELLE PAUL

Harlequin Books

TORONTO • NEW YORK • LONDON
AMSTERDAM • PARIS • SYDNEY • HAMBURG
STOCKHOLM • ATHENS • TOKYO • MILAN

Published June 1984

ISBN 0-373-25113-0

Printed in Canada

1

SIOBHAN RYAN looked into the dressing room mirror, her somewhat startled smile turning into a wide grin. "You'll never get used to looking like that, Vona Butler, known to television viewers as Siobhan Ryan." Her hand lifted to the black silk, skintight jump suit that she wore in her role as a sexpot in the weekly soap opera, "Day By Day."

She pushed her hand through her hair when she loosened it from the chignon and shook her head. It was true. The lissome blonde with the violet eyes bore little resemblance to the brassy redhead who had worked in a diner outside New Paltz, New York, just two years ago. She had worked days and gone to classes nights on the slow road to getting a degree in theater arts, with the intention of becoming an actress.

Siobhan's hand shook as she lifted the alcohol-soaked cotton to her face to clean off the last of her makeup. "Now, instead of being the waitress I was when I started college at seventeen, I'm an actress on TV at the ripe old age of twenty-four. . . ." Her laugh was shaky as she tried not to think of the evening ahead, when she would be reintroduced to James Kendall Deerfield.

Since learning of the impending meeting, she had stuffed the idea of seeing James Kendall Deerfield again—called "Jake" by friend and enemy—in the back pocket of her mind, finding comfort in learning her lines as Raine, the part she played, and rehearsing the show.

"The moment of truth," Siobhan muttered to her image. "Why did I tell Hughy I would see him?" she asked the mirror.

"Because Jake would have steamrollered any objection Hughy gave him," the mirror replied.

Sitting back in the straight chair in front of the dressing table, she put a shaking hand up to her mouth and tried to force herself to rise, remove her robe and get dressed. The knock at the door made her jump. It wouldn't be him! He was going to meet her at the restaurant. That had been the stipulation.

"Siobhan, Siobhan, are you in there?"

She exhaled, feeling her calves turn to water as she rose, went to the door, unlocked and opened it. "Come in, Hughy." She didn't look at the sandy-haired man of medium height and weight, whose cleverness was masked behind the fresh-faced preppie look he didn't even try to change.

He bounced into the room, his high-test energy level rarely allowing him to walk. "Hiding out in here?"

"Yes." She looked at him in the mirror, then slumped back into the chair again. "He'll recognize me."

Hughy pressed his lips together and slammed his hands into the pockets of the dress jacket in a way that would have given his Madison Avenue tailor acute heartburn. "Jake is sharp. I don't deny it, but I don't think he'll connect the snippy, gum-chewing waitress from New Paltz whose hair was the color of cheap copper with svelte, blond Siobhan Ryan, smash-hit newcomer to television." Hughy's elfin grin brought a fleeting smile to Siobhan's face. "Besides he isn't an ogre, Siobhan. He's considered a Good Samaritan—even by some of his enemies."

"Who are legion, no doubt." Siobhan said in a cracked voice, reapplying her lip gloss for the third time.

"He donated a huge personal check to spearhead a drive that enabled employees in Coaltown to purchase their foundry from the owners and keep themselves working." Hughy continued as though she hadn't spoken. "He travels far and wide to take part in Special Olympics activities." He grinned at her. "He's been called 'the industrialist with a heart' by a well-known slush columnist in town."

"He looks more like Darth Vader to me." Siobhan could feel her jaw thrust outward when Hughy laughed.

"Most women consider his tall, dark good looks very sexy." Hughy shrugged. "When the two of us started dabbling in the media, Jake was approached to be an actor in a series. Sort of a new Burt Reynolds."

"Twaddle," Siobhan said crisply, ignoring the quivering in her knees as Jake's image rose in front of her eyes.

Hughy leaned over and patted her shoulder. "I tell you he won't know you. You were just a girl he flirted with in a diner two years ago."

"Who pushed his hand into a lemon pie!" Siobhan rose to her feet, ignoring a laughing Hughy, tearing the makeup cape from her neck and going around the screen to change into the outfit she had chosen to wear for the evening.

As she threw her discarded robe over the top, Hughy retrieved it and placed it on a hanger, to be put in the curtained closet.

"Are we still dining with him at Lutèce?" Her voice was muffled behind the screen.

"Yes. And he's damned anxious to meet you. He called me twice today. Once, to see if I would make it an earlier time. The second time to find out what color you were wearing. I told him that we couldn't make it earlier and that I didn't know what color—" Hughy stopped speaking, his mouth dropping open as she stepped from behind the curtain and twirled in front of him, the small dressing room spoiling the grand effect. "That color is two shades deeper than your eyes. And in satin! You look like one of Lucifer's daughters with your hair in that wild free style. You don't often let it hang down past your shoulders like that. It's so wavy and thick." Hughy looked at her and shook his head.

Siobhan laughed, throwing back her head, the combination of fear and elation at seeing Jake Deerfield after more than two years making her giddy. She had never forgotten him. She could never tell Hughy that she had dreamed of Jake, and that in her dream.... She shook her head to clear it of yesterday, then walked to the full-length, three-way mirror and studied her image, hoping that Hughy couldn't see into the turmoil of her mind. She knew that her outfit was outrageous, the grape color of the long tunic and tight pants a wild foil for her violet eyes. Her coloring was the reason she had been chosen for the part of Raine, the vamp of the highly rated nighttime TV series. Her streaky red-blond hair didn't call for violet eyes, and many people did a double-take when they first looked at her. It was grimly humorous to her that the brassy red she had dyed her hair when she was younger had fitted her coloring better, or so she always thought.

As a rule, she didn't wear avant-garde clothes and mostly wore dresses, feeling that her tall, five foot nine inch figure looked better in skirts and gowns. Tonight she had the need to be elusive, bolstered, camouflaged. She wished she could have worn a mask and cape.

"What are you thinking, O purple lady, as you admire yourself in the mirror?" Hughy asked from over her shoulder. In her heels, she was an inch taller than he. But she would be shadowed by Jake's six foot five frame. Jake—whose heavy-lidded eyes rarely laughed. To Siobhan he was a hard man, despite what Hughy said about his philanthropies. Born with a fine name and wealth, he had still gone out and built a computer empire; then, before turning thirty, he had hacked out a corner of the media business and was now considered a knowledgeable producer.

"Perhaps the color is a bit outré." Her brow furrowed. "It's called grape."

"Wear it. You look sensational. Who would ever dream that a Mexican serape could be designed in satin." Hughy grinned.

"It's a tunic." Siobhan instructed, trying to smile.

"With skintight pants, gold buttons at the ankle—and those shoes! Where did you get purple lizard?"

"Grape." Siobhan corrected absently, shifting the tunic top that fastened at each shoulder with a gold clip, then draped on the bias down the front so that the hem was diagonally uneven. The dolman sleeves looked as though they were part of the serape unless she lifted her arms high.

"Quite frankly, I have never seen you so covered. Sleeves to the wrist, legs wrapped to the ankles, neckline high. It's a wonder you didn't wrap a scarf around your neck."

"Maybe I should," she muttered, affixing the triple circles of gold to her ears. The circles hung free of each other so that when she moved, they twisted and turned and caught the light, refracting it back onto her cheeks and adding to the feverish violet glitter of her eyes.

She grasped a gold wrist purse and whirled to face her friend. "Shall we go?"

"So said Marie Antoinette to the person helping her into the tumbrel cart that would carry her to Madame La Guillotine," Hughy intoned, bowing slightly, then opening the door. "Are you sure you won't need a wrap?"

"No. It's a little cool this evening, but it's spring in New York. I don't want to wear a coat." Siobhan bit her lip, realizing she was babbling a bit. She did not want to see Jake Deerfield! She could have gone on for the rest of her life and not seen Jake Deerfield and been happy. She pushed the thought of when she had first met him from her mind and accompanied Hughy out into the crisp coldness of a Manhattan evening in late March. She shivered a bit. It wasn't from the cold.

Hughy hurried her across the sidewalk to where his car was parked. Bundling her inside, he went around the front and climbed behind the wheel, leaning on it after he started the car. "Siobhan, I nearly died when he told me he wanted to meet you—that he'd seen you in the bit part of Mary on the 'Olympia' show," Hughy whispered.

"I know. We were fools to think we'd never run into him again. He does own the larger share of the network that carries my show," Siobhan sighed.

"Damn him. Wouldn't you think he'd have enough to do with World Computers without dipping his fingers into television?"

"He was the one that started you. Or at least, that's what you told me." Siobhan rested a tired head on the upholstered seat.

"True. When we met you, I had just finished my second stint as a producer and realized that I was hooked on the media." Hughy admitted. "What a horror you were." He laughed and started the car when Siobhan punched him on the arm. "A skinny, underfed urchin of twenty-two with eyes too big for her body."

The drive to the restaurant took longer than it should have because of the traffic, but neither of them complained.

When they reached the doors to the restaurant, Hughy paused. "Remember, if he does decide to eat the two of us, I taste better broiled."

"Very amusing." Siobhan's throat was desert dry as they entered and approached the maitre d'.

"Mr. Deerfield's party," Hughy announced.

Then they were crossing the room. Hughy spoke to acquaintances. Siobhan looked at the back of the attendant ushering them to a secluded table. She ignored the curious glances of the people who spoke to Hughy, concentrating every effort on not being sick. She watched a dark-suited man uncoil himself from a chair and look toward her. It shocked her that he looked almost the same. Did he have those graying sideburns two years ago? Was his face so hard-bitten, so cynical? If she recognized him, wouldn't he know her?

She wanted to run! Escape! As she and the maitre d' approached him, he seemed to resemble a giant bat in his dinner suit, his coal black hair echoing the sheen of the silky fabric, his midnight-blue eyes having the look of onyx. For all his height he moved smoothly, his wide shoulders elegant, his hands narrow and strong, his eyebrows the same deep black as his hair. She knew the carved chin would need shaving twice a day, and that the light bristling effect of the skin was erotic in the extreme. She pinched her nails into her palms to steady herself, and to clear her thoughts of yesterday.

"Siobhan Ryan." The resonant timbre of the voice was unchanged. "I've been wanting to meet you." He put out his hands and closed them over the one she offered him. "Hughy, how are you?" There was a hard glint to the smile he gave his friend and Siobhan knew that he hadn't forgotten the many previous times Hughy had put him off meeting her.

Hughy reached around Siobhan with his hand and held it there until Jake released her hand and shook his. "Good to see you, Jake. I don't see you at the gym anymore."

"I've been in and out of the country. Miss Ryan, won't you sit here?"

"Thank you." Siobhan coughed to clear the raspiness from her throat. As soon as she was seated with the men on either side of her, she reached for the yard-high menu proffered by the waiter's assistant and hid behind it. She was startled to have the scrolled cardboard removed from her hands.

"I took the liberty of ordering for us. The prawns are excellent here and Hughy tells me that seafood is a favorite of yours." His smile lifted that sensual mouth, making Siobhan take a deep breath.

"Yes. I like seafood. Thank you." Her gaze slid toward Hughy.

"Ah...yes. How is the computer business, Jake? I must say I'm glad I didn't take you up on your offer to come into World Computers with you. I have enough to do keeping an eye on Siobhan and the few shows I do." Hughy cleared his throat, swirled the ice around his glass of gin and lime, then took a sip, eyeing Jake over the rim.

"Computer business is fine, and since we work rather closely on DeerPren Productions, I needn't inform you about that," Jake clipped back barely looking at Hughy. His eyes were fixed on Siobhan. "I saw you do Mary for the 'Olympia' show. Very good."

When she looked at him and smiled, she saw an arrested look in his eyes, a flicker of surprise. "Thank you." Siobhan felt like a puppet. She couldn't think of one rational conversational gambit. Her brain tried out a few opening lines like *Remember me? I'm the girl you called a sow's ear when Hughy suggested that I had nice bones in my face and might fit the part of Elaine in "Rainbow." Surprise, surprise. Or, Hi there, I'm the waitress who pushed your hand in the lemon meringue pie, and then went to bed with you just because you asked me. Damn my stupidity.*

Siobhan heard Hughy cough and blinked at him.

"Jake asked you how you liked the part of Raine in 'Day by Day.'" Hughy's face had a tight, strained look, his pale hazel eyes more protuberant than usual.

She stared at her white wine on ice and wondered why she hadn't ordered Saratoga water and lime, the drink she enjoyed. "Yes, it's a good part and Del Krantz is a good director." She felt her lips tremble in a smile when she looked at Hughy, then bit her bottom lip to steady it. "Hughy is an excellent producer."

"How nice for you!" Jake barked, sarcasm blistering his tone, his eyes shooting from Siobhan to Hughy and back again.

That aristocratic ass, she simmered inside, *how he looks down on everyone!* "Perhaps it would be better if we discussed you, Mr. Deerfield. I'm sure that would give us far more...scope." Although she kept her tone as neutral as possible, she could tell that Hughy knew she was angry by the way he shifted in his chair, lifting

his glass to his mouth, then putting it back down on the
table without drinking.

As timely as the bell in a boxing match, the waiter
appeared with the dinners, saving them from a long,
incendiary moment.

The succulent prawns, looking more like lobster tails
because of their size, had the aroma of black pepper and
lemon.

Siobhan's appetite, a throwback to the hungry days
when she had subsisted on one meal a day at the diner,
surfaced at once. No matter how disturbed or rattled
she was, nothing ever got in the way of eating. Yet she
stayed almost as stick-thin as she had been in college.
When she saw others push away plates of luscious food
and say they weren't hungry, she would bite her tongue
to keep from railing at them. No matter how bad things
became, when good food was put in front of Siobhan
Ryan, she ate.

Hughy, who usually chattered while eating, concentrated silently on his food as well.

Though Jake Deerfield ate, he also drank, refilling his
glass from the iced bottle in the bucket near his elbow.

"Sure, Jake, I'll have more champagne. Good."
Hughy took his refilled glass and gulped down the wine.

"None for me, thanks." Siobhan put her index finger
on the rim of her glass, looking right into those coal-
blue eyes, ready to rip his face with her nails as the hot
lava of memory stirred in her. Damn him to the hottest
fires in Hell.

He stared back at her. "You're quite a fiery woman,
aren't you, Siobhan Ryan. Beautiful, too." The smile
was hard and the glitter in those eyes matched the anger
she was fighting to mask.

"No, thank you, I don't care for dessert." Siobhan

spoke to the waiter, ignoring what Jake had said to her. Then she looked at Hughy. "I do have a meeting in the morning with Morey...."

Hughy pushed back his chair, looking relieved. "Right. I have to get Siobhan home..." he began.

Jake rose. "I have an early meeting myself. But I'm sure that we could stop at Dominie's for a nightcap." It wasn't a request.

"Ah...all right. We can do that, Siobhan—then I'll get you home."

"I could always take Siobhan home in *my* car." Jake nodded good-night to the maitre d', somehow intruding his way between Hughy and Siobhan and taking her arm.

Outside, the March wind whistled down into the stone and glass caves of Manhattan, making Siobhan shudder.

"My car is over here." Jake threw his arm over her shoulder and guided her to a Ferrari parked in a No Parking zone. "We'll meet you at Dominie's, Hughy." He had hustled her into the car before she could protest, an open-mouthed Hughy staring at Siobhan's shocked face.

She tried the door.

"It's locked on the wheel for safety," he informed her, engaging the gears and pulling sharply away from the curb.

"I do not like speed," she said through her teeth. "Nor do I appreciate being kidnapped when my escort is in another vehicle."

"He's just behind us." The tone was flat, but anger vibrated through the car.

"Why the antipathy, Miss Ryan? Is it wise to show it to the man who wields the power?"

Siobhan took a deep breath. "If you're threatening me, Mr. Deerfield, then fire me. It won't be the first time."

"Damn you!" he swung the car so viciously she was thrown against her seat belt like a rag doll. "I don't threaten. I do what has to be done. Nor do I accept impertinence from people who work for me."

"I'll talk to my lawyer about getting out of my contract," she hissed.

Pulling into Dominie's driveway, he slammed on the brakes. "You will not!" he snarled.

She tore frantically at the seat belt buckled at her waist, her breath rasping in the sudden silence.

Hands reached out to grasp her shaking ones, holding them tight for a moment. "Don't. Stop," Jake told her, coming up to take hold of her chin. "That got out of hand. I'm sorry."

Siobhan quivered, her skin rippling in tremors.

"Truce." His fingers tightened for a moment on her chin. "Look at me, Siobhan."

"Hey . . ." Hughy banged on the window of the passenger side. "Is anything wrong?"

Siobhan pulled free of Jake's hand and turned to look out at Hughy, mutely begging him to open the door.

He rattled the handle, looking from Siobhan to Jake. Muttering an imprecation, Jake touched the switch on the wheel to open the door. Siobhan scrambled out, almost into Hughy's arms.

"What the hell happened?" Hughy held her by the arms as Jake came around the car.

"Nothing." Jake slipped his hand through her arm and turned her toward him, pulling her away from Hughy. "We had an argument, but . . . ."

"Mr. Deerfield and I feel that my contract with . . ."

Siobhan began, fully aware that she couldn't last in a contest of wills with Jake Deerfield. Better to lose her job on television and have to start again, than have a verbal wrestling match with him every time they met.

"Stop it, Siobhan," Jake growled, walking her toward the entrance to Dominie's, its marquee flapping in the wind. "There will be no change in your contract status."

She jerked her arm free and turned to face him, her chin up. "I will not verbally spar with you. Nor will I—"

Jake reached over and put his two fingers over her lips. "Truce. Remember?" He took her arm again, pulling her close to his side, his body sheltering her from the wind as Hughy opened the door.

Again a maitre d' came forward, but this time there was a woman at his side.

"Good evening, Jean. Hello, Dominie. I brought friends. I think you know Mr. Prentice. And this—" Jake leaned down and let his mouth brush Siobhan's forehead "—this is Siobhan Ryan, rising star of—"

"I know who Miss Ryan is." The cigarette-roughened voice of the woman was decibels lower than Siobhan expected from the mannequin-like creature who welcomed them. "I watch 'Day by Day.' Wouldn't miss it." She laughed at Siobhan's look. "I can read your mind, Siobhan Ryan. You're wondering how a woman who looks like an aging Dolly Parton could sound like Lauren Bacall. Right?"

The laugh bubbled up from inside Siobhan and escaped, the sound of it turning heads and bringing smiles to the faces of people around them.

Jake stared at her, long and hard, his mouth oddly twisted.

Siobhan felt the fine hairs on her body lift in alarm.

"Is something wrong?" she swallowed. "You look angry again."

Jake walked close behind her as she followed Dominie to a table. "It has nothing to do with you. Your laugh reminded me of something. . . ."

"Bad?" She took the seat held for her by the waiter, keeping her eyes averted from Jake.

"Let's say it recalls a bad woman." His cynical smile touched her for a moment before he looked at Dominie and invited her to join their table. He didn't see Siobhan chew at her lower lip.

Bastard! She thought. He had remembered her as Vona Butler for a moment. He had told her once that he liked her laugh. *Do you recall what you thought she was, Jake?* she asked him silently. *A trick, and not an expensive one at that.* She jumped when she felt Hughy nudge her, and glanced at Jake, whose head was bent as he listened to Dominie telling him something. Though the music was good and not too loud, it still impeded easy conversation. She looked at Hughy.

"What went on in the car? When I first saw your face, I thought sure he had. . . ." He stopped speaking as though he felt Jake turn and look at him. Hughy smiled at his old university friend, then looked back at Siobhan. "Well?" he hissed.

She shook her head. "He didn't recognize me, but I think something about me bothers him," she whispered back, then felt Jake's eyes on her. "I'll have a grasshopper, I think." She spoke in more normal tones to Hughy.

"You don't drink," Hughy muttered, nodding to the hovering waiter.

"I could always have a long, cool hemlock on the rocks," Siobhan pointed out in honeyed tones.

"Maybe even a double," Hughy muttered back, after

giving their order to the waiter. "Why the hell is he glaring at me now? He hardly let me speak to you through dinner."

"I thought you and Jake were best friends," she murmured to Hughy, smiling at Dominie and letting the smile slip Jake's way without really looking at him.

Jake rose and came around to her chair, pulling it out and taking hold of her arm. "Dance with me."

"I don't dance," Siobhan stated as he marched her out to the floor, then turned her in his arms, one of his hands at the base of her spine, the other moving gently between her shoulder blades.

"Why did you lie about dancing? You move like an angel," Jake whispered into her ear.

"I didn't lie. I was going to say that I don't dance with people I've just met," she improvised.

"Liar," Jake crooned, tightening his arms when she would have pulled back. "Stop battling me and listen to the music."

Siobhan threw words around her mind like a handball in a court, but nothing tumbled from her throat. She listened to the music, enjoying the slow beguine beat, until she became aware of his body moving against hers, the strong muscular thighs in caressing rhythm against her, the hands massaging her back. She felt herself respond and react, her hands gently gripping his shoulders, her body fitting to his like a hand to a glove. When the music changed to an even slower tune, they were barely moving, Jake's head moved down toward hers as though his body would curtain hers, block her from the view of any other.

"I want to see you again."

Siobhan's mind was an empty room with no windows.

"We'll have dinner and talk, just the two of us."

"Work—" Her scrambling mind found a word, making her sag with relief.

"You don't work twenty-four hours a day," Jake informed her, his tones soothing.

"Hard work never hurt anyone," she panted, trying to re-form her gelatinous mind.

"All work and no play make Jill a dull girl," Jake clichéd, a laugh in his voice.

"Perceptive of you," Siobhan noted as she tried to look over her shoulder at Hughy.

"Never mind Hughy. He's talking to Dominie." Jake's voice pounded the words like a sledge hitting rock.

"He's my friend," she insisted, feeling Jake's leg rub hers.

"I'll be your friend," Jake breathed in her ear.

"Too tall," Siobhan squeaked, her bones disintegrating, her heart valves knotting.

"You are one silly lady, do you know that?" Jake chuckled.

Siobhan nodded.

As the music stopped this time, an MC came out onto the tiny stage and beckoned the people to take their seats, indicating that he had a treat in store for them.

While Siobhan looked on the MC as a savior, Jake sent him venomous looks that would have frightened the Sphinx.

When they sat down, Siobhan reached out for the glass in front of her and drained the pale green frothy mixture, earning a horrified look from Hughy. Jake kissed her cheek and excused himself for a moment.

"Let's go home—now," Siobhan suddenly surged to her feet, gave a shaky smile at a knowing Dominie and pulled at Hughy's arm. "I'm tired."

"You shouldn't let Jake get to you, Siobhan," Dominie rasped, tipping the ash from her cigarette into the ashtray. "He's a very tough man but a good one."

"Said the frog who gave the scorpion a ride across the water..." Siobhan babbled, "...and when the frog said, 'Why did you sting me? Now I'll die and you'll drown,' the scorpion said, 'it's my nature.'"

"I think she has a fever," Hughy explained. "Tell Jake." Then he hurried after a charging Siobhan. "Wait...."

"Can't," she gasped. "I am not going to spend one more moment in that Ferrari of his." She shivered in the night air, shifting her weight from one foot to the other as she waited for Hughy to unlock his Mercedes. "Hurry." She urged once they were in the car.

"For God's sake," Hughy pulled away from the club, Siobhan looking through the small back window. "He isn't Jack the Ripper, you know."

"That's what you think," she muttered, huddling down in her seat as Hughy drove through the Manhattan night to the apartment house where they each had an apartment. Hughy owned the building.

As Siobhan got out from the car in the underground garage, she took a deep breath. "I am glad that's over and I never have to see him again." The sound of the words in the garage had an echo that bolstered her. She didn't have to see him again! He didn't own her! She felt better just saying that to herself. She smiled at Hughy in the elevator taking them first to her floor—the fifth, then to his floor—the eighth.

As usual, he accompanied her to her door and waited until she had turned on the lights in her living room before saying good-night. "I'll see you at rehearsal tomorrow," he told her, then kissed her on the cheek.

Siobhan yawned and nodded. Her time to rise was much earlier than his, as she was due at the studio at eight. He would come down about ten or eleven, depending on the meetings he had.

Siobhan smiled as she looked around her small apartment with its lounge, kitchen, bedroom and bath. It was more room than she'd ever had at home when she'd lived with her parents, four brothers and two sisters. For a moment, the pang of missing them was there. The Butlers had been a close family and after her adored father died, things had been very tough for them. Siobhan, being the second oldest, had had to get a job as well as double up her courses in high school so that she could graduate a year early at sixteen. She had also signed up for night courses at the university.

She had commuted into New Paltz from their small farm on the outskirts every day, catching a ride from a neighbor.

When her mother had met Andrew Selkirk from Australia and married him, all the Butlers had been happy because Andrew was as good and kind a man as their father had been. Then Siobhan took an apartment in town.

When she was nineteen her stepfather moved his new family back to Australia and the sheep station that had been in his family. Her mother was happy in Australia and so were her brothers and sisters. Siobhan sighed, missing them, but figuring she would have enough money next year to fly out to the island continent.

It was when she had been on her own for just under three years that she had met Jake Deerfield and Hughy Prentice.

Shaking her head to scatter the memories of that time, she went to her tiny kitchen and put the kettle on for tea. Herbal tea often had a relaxing effect on her frazzled nerves at the end of a long day of rehearsing.

She changed into a night robe and soft slippers, then padded through to the lounge to drink her orange spice brew on the couch. Yawning, she put her head back and let the warm liquid do its work.

The jangle of the phone shrilly demanded her attention. She went into the bedroom and picked up the receiver. "Yes, Hughy, what is it?" she yawned.

"That answers my first question. You're not sleeping with him." Jake's drawl was a sensual hum in her ear. She shivered, feeling the goose bumps on her arms and legs. "Don't hang up, Siobhan. I'll just have to call back again."

"I really don't do business at this hour . . . and since I don't date anyone involved in my work, I can't see what we have to say to one another." Her voice cracked on the last words.

"No? I can think of a dozen things we should discuss. For starters, why you would walk out of a club and leave me."

"I was tired, Mr. Deerfield. I'm sure Dominie gave you my message." Siobhan gripped the phone as though it were the only anchor to earth she had.

"Have lunch with me tomorrow." The words traveled along the wire like an electronic spear.

"No!" she shot back. "I'll be working all day . . . fittings . . . script conference—"

"I'll take care of it." Jake interrupted.

"No! I need to be at all the things I mentioned."

"You mean no one takes a lunch hour in that company?"

"They do, but sometimes it's just sandwiches as we work," Siobhan clarified, in all truth. "Now, Mr. Deerfield, I really am tired."

"Good night, lovely Siobhan. See you."

The phone buzzed in her hand as she still held it to her ear. "Good night," she murmured, cradling the phone, then going through all the mechanical checks she did each night on retiring: stove, turn down heat, check doors, windows, tighten faucets that might drip. Most of her checks were not necessary, but the years of living on her own, when extra safety precautions were a way of life, had left their mark on her.

She climbed into bed, sure that she would sleep. She had developed an almost infallible way of dealing with insomnia on the rare occasions when she suffered from it. She totally relaxed her body, starting with her toes and working slowly up her body to her eyelids, which she would close thinking of black...black velvet, black satin, black silk, black sleep....

Her eyes popped open. Tonight it didn't work. Her mind was like an over-stuffed drawer that couldn't be closed. Thoughts spilled from the cracks, and grew as they did so, puffing and swelling. Scenes from long-ago yesterdays filled her mind. She could smell the burnt grease on the griddle, see the steam rise from the hot-table, the red lamps adding to the overpowering heat as she ran back and forth from counter to customers in the understaffed diner. She remembered.

"Vona, get the lead out!" bellowed Clarence, the overfed owner of Clarence's Diner, supervising the whole operation in a greasy multi-colored waistcoat that was a macabre menu of past meals served at the diner.

"Yeah, yeah," Vona panted, her gum-chewing speed increasing as she raced around the hot room, head down, intent only on getting her trays onto the tables without spilling, then racing back for another load.

"Easy, Red, you'll break something." An amused drawl rolled over her like summer rain.

Vona Butler, aged twenty-two, tall and thin, raised her heavily painted eyes from the cutlery she was arranging to observe Bedroom Eyes, as she dubbed the midnight-blue eyes running over her confidently.

"I'm used to this," she answered him, unwilling to look away from that hard-planed face, topped by slightly curling black hair.

"Vona, move it!" Clarence yelled.

"Yeah, yeah, I'm coming." She was able to look away from that face for a second.

"You'd better get back to work, sweetie," Midnight-blue Eyes warned her. "Here comes the chain gang warden."

"Are you passing through?" Vona rushed her words, one eye on the rampaging Clarence.

"Visiting the family home a few miles from here with my friend, Hughy." Bedroom Eyes informed her.

"Hi," Friend Hughy had interpolated.

Vona took vague note of the friend named Hughy. "Hi," she said, still watching Tall, Dark and Sexy.

"Vona, move it," Clarence brayed, breaking the marshmallow aura around her and snapping her back into the breakneck speed that made up her day.

When she was passing their table some moments later, both men were so engrossed in their conversation that they didn't notice her. But she overheard Bedroom Eyes talking to his friend. "I tell you Hughy, she's just not a girl who would do well in television. She has no style and I'm sure no talent. She's just a gum-chewing broad who probably turns a trick for a buck."

Vona felt as though her shoes were nailed to the floor as she listened.

The man called Hughy glared at his friend. "If you weren't so damned hung over from last night, you wouldn't be talking this way. And I disagree, not just about her looks, but about her personality as well. She has sensitive eyes...and...and great cheekbones. That fragile, Nordic look is very appealing and, I'll bet, photogenic. Copper-haired waitress she may be but she has potential," he insisted.

They were discussing her! Vona bit her underlip. Damn them! Scalding temper built within her as she continued to eavesdrop, passing back and forth near them.

"Come on, Hughy. You're a dreamer! You think she could act? That she has talent? Oh my aching head...." Bedroom Eyes massaged his forehead with one hand.

After delivering pancakes, poached eggs on rye toast, three coffees and two danishes to another table, she stood near theirs, listening to two strangers dissect her.

"Listen to me, Hughy, my friend, I haven't been in television much longer than you, but I think I can recognize a bomb when I see it. And that brassy redhead is a bomb, even if she does have violet eyes." He squeezed his temples with his fingers. "You can't make a silk purse out of a sow's ear. That babe is a sow's ear."

Vona saw red stars and planets in front of her eyes as she carefully set down her tray on an empty table and picked up one of the plates of lemon meringue pie from under the transparent cover on the counter. Chin high, she walked back to table number four, taking deep breaths every step of the way.

She plunked down the pie, ignoring the inquiring looks on the faces of the two men. "Have some dessert." Vona grabbed Jake's right hand and pushed it down into the gooey meringue as hard as she could. "Sow's ear, am

I? You silver-spooned ass!" She strode away from the table, not looking back when she heard the chair crash to the floor and Bedroom Eyes roar to his feet, his cursing varied and colorful.

"Vona!" Clarence thundered, looking from her to the fiasco at table four. Then, he stampeded over to try to placate the customer with sticky lemon and egg white covering his hand. From the kitchen, she watched as Apollo and his friend left the restaurant—Apollo swearing and his friend choking back laughter.

"If it wasn't that you've been here for awhile, you dumb broad, I'd throw you out that front door...." Clarence fumed at her later as she walked through the kitchen to the small changing room in the back.

"That, plus the fact that you couldn't get anyone to work for as little money as I do and do the work of three...." Vona shot back, hearing the cook and his helper titter. She was ready to toss in the towel anyway.

Perhaps that was what Clarence saw in her eyes, because though he fussed for several minutes longer, he said nothing to her about losing her job.

That night when she went to her classes in "Origin of History Writing" and "English Logistics," she forced her mind from thoughts of the stranger with the midnight-blue eyes and concentrated on her work. Her total, grim attack on the books kept her three point eight average steady. Vona was no genius, unless a capacity for hard work could be called genius. "Then I'm a whiz," she muttered to herself as she flipped through her notebook, jotting down Professor Jenkins's remarks on the ability of the Ancient Greeks to describe the happenings of their time under the cloak of mythology. When the professor mentioned Apollo, Vona lost the thread of his words and pictured the sardonic smile of the man at table four.

Back at home, she cracked the books until well after midnight. Then she checked the locks on her windows and doors, jamming a chair under the door handle as an added safety measure. Not two weeks before, someone had rattled her door and tried to force it. Living above Mr. Dianetti's store hardly offered the best accommodation, but it was all she could afford, so she took every step to protect herself. She had been doing that since she was nineteen and on her own. She considered every aspect of each move she made, knowing that as a girl living alone, she could be a prime target for the unsavory characters that sometimes roam a university town.

That night she dreamed that Apollo made love to her, that he held her, kissed her and lay down with her on her hideabed, his hands roving her body. She woke clutching her pillow, cold perspiration dampening her body.

The next day she was back on the job at six o'clock, wearing her pink dress and pink frilly apron, frayed and thin from countless washings, but fresh and clean just the same—a glaring contrast to her brassy red locks. She had tied her hair in a pony tail with a snood net over it.

She was plowing through her work as usual, her legs pumping back and forth across the room, from the hot counter to the tables and back again.

When she stopped at table four, pad and pencil in hand, she didn't look at the customers.

"Hello, sweetie. Still running, I see." The not-so-velvet drawl crawled up her spine.

Vona stiffened, her chin coming up, her eyes hooked by those midnight-blue ones. He had come to have her fired, she deduced fatalistically. "Good morning, sir," she swallowed.

"Instead of the lemon pie today, I'll have eggs over easy and sausages, with rye toast and home fries." He glinted at her, his nostrils flaring slightly as he leaned toward her.

"Coffee, sir?" Vona leaned as far back from him as she could.

"Of course, angel," he hissed, watching her gulp. His finger came out and curled over the top of her frilly apron. "Tell me your name."

Vona wanted to tell him to go to hell, but her tongue stuck to the roof of her mouth. "Vona Butler," she had whispered.

"See, Hughy, she has a name. This is Hughy. I'm Jake."

Vona blinked at the friend, whom she hadn't noticed until Jake mentioned his name. "Hi." She couldn't seem to clear the huskiness from her throat.

She raced to the china-table and retrieved two cups and saucers, grasped the pot with three free fingers and spun back to the table, pouring the coffee without spilling a drop in the saucers.

They came in like that for five days and each time Apollo seemed to stare at Vona more. He was in her thoughts all the time. She knew that he hadn't forgotten the lemon pie incident, though it was never alluded to by either of them.

Often she heard them discuss casting for a television show, and their search for talent. But as much as she wanted to ask them if she could audition, she could never summon up the nerve.

One morning when she went to take the order at table four, Apollo wasn't there.

"Good morning," Hughy smiled. "We met formally over lemon pie, I think."

Vona groaned. "Don't let my boss hear you. He doesn't let a day go by without mentioning it at least once."

"I think my friend deserved it." Hughy smiled at her in such a disarming way that Vona smiled back.

"I heard you say that you thought I had good bones . . ." she ventured.

"I do." Hughy nodded once.

"I'm studying theater arts, and I'd like to audition for you sometime," Vona braced herself, waiting for the string of excuses he would offer.

"All right. I'm casting for a show, and there could be a part for you." Hughy grinned at her. "You'll catch flies if you don't close your mouth." He handed her a card with his name, address and phone number and told her to come to town the following Tuesday.

Vona scraped together bus fare for the trip to Manhattan and went to the audition. She was accepted for a small walk-on part. Then Hughy took her to a tiny French restaurant and they talked until it was time for Vona to catch her bus.

"Don't forget, Vona. Talk to your dean about transferring your credits down here, and then we'll get on with the other stuff." Hughy looked up at her as she stared from the bus window, and pointed at his head. "And no more color in the hair."

That had been the beginning. With Hughy's help and guidance, she had switched to university in Manhattan, sought and found lessons in aerobic dance, modeling, makeup. He had coached her in so many things, like conversational French and choosing the right wine, that their friendship had deepened, but not in a romantic way. Finally had come the part of Raine in "Day By Day."

IN THOSE TWO YEARS, Siobhan had tried not to think of Jake. Hughy knew she disliked him, and though he had tried at first to convince her that Jake Deerfield was a better man than he had acted that day in the diner, Siobhan would not accept that. By tacit agreement Jake Deerfield had become a conversational no-no.

She never told Hughy that she had seen Jake that evening on her return to New Paltz from New York. She had never told Hughy that Jake had come to the diner that evening, that she had gone out with him later, that she had gone to Deerfield Hall with him, that they had.... No! No! She wouldn't remember that! She couldn't!

Now, Siobhan lay in bed and tried to sleep, her body chilled with perspiration despite the hot bath she had taken. "No, no, I will not let him get to me again. Damn him for invading my thoughts for two years." Siobhan gritted her teeth, the sheet clutched up to her chin as she remembered the many times she would be preparing for a part when the memory of their time together returned. What would Jake Deerfield think of her now? Would Jake Deerfield think she had given a great performance?

"Damn you to the hottest fires of hell, Jake Deerfield. I will not give one cotton damn what you think about anything I do. Get out of my brain. Stay out of my life." She closed her eyes, willing herself into the black well of sleep.

2

THE NEXT DAY when Siobhan rose to shower at six, she frowned at her mirror image in the bathroom. "Those gray patches under your eyes will not photograph too well," she muttered, splashing cold water on her face for five minutes in an effort to remove some of the swelling under her eyes.

Her makeup application took much longer as she applied all her knowledge to erasing the tell-tale traces of a restless night.

She was late and missed her usual bus. Rather than stand and wait for the next one, she began walking, taking deep breaths of the cold, crisp March air into her lungs. Even with her briefcase on one shoulder and her clothes and makeup case hanging from the other, she made good time, her long legs stretching out in front of her, welcoming the exercise.

She had dressed in a long-waisted sailor dress with a short pleated skirt, the deep blue of the material matching the double-breasted pea coat she wore. She was hatless, but the big coat collar well protected her head. The wind behind her affected only the long expanse of leg covered by white stockings and flat-heeled navy blue shoes.

She was panting slightly when she hailed a bus not six blocks from her destination, the two shoulder bags suddenly feeling like ton weights.

When she walked into the studio reception on the tenth floor of station WEW, Flora, the woman who blockaded the inner sanctum from outsiders, looked up at her and smiled. "You look ten years old in that outfit with that braid hanging down your back, and all that wonderful color in your cheeks. What did you do? Run up Fifth Avenue?"

"Almost," Siobhan grinned, feeling a good tiredness, some of the cobwebs in her mind disappearing.

"Better get in there. The Great One has a bee in his bonnet today...." Flora raised thin brows and rolled her eyes.

Siobhan nodded and groaned. Del Krantz was a dynamo when he was working and he spun everyone who worked for him in his special vortex. "Are they in the conference room?"

"I don't think so. I think Del has everyone in his office."

All morning the meeting dragged on, the new idea that Del had for the successful series proving to be unworkable the many times they tried it.

When a halt was called for lunch, Siobhan felt as though she had perspired off ten pounds. She opened her eyes and sat up in her chair when she felt the touch on her arm. "Oh, Hughy! Were you listening?"

He nodded. "I was here for most of it. Del is a genius, but he does wring out his actors."

"True." Siobhan sighed, patting the chair next to her.

"Have you sent out for sandwiches?" Hughy asked, taking the towel from her hands and wiping her forehead.

"No—she's having lunch with me." Jake said from behind them, making Siobhan's head snap as she looked up and back.

He was upside down in her sight, his smile looking bizarre. "Ah, hello." she managed. When she would have lowered her head, she saw his mouth descending toward her too fast for her to move. When his lips brushed hers lightly, her stomach contracted as though she had just dropped down the steepest track of the roller coaster.

"Good morning, Siobhan," he said, then looked at Hughy, not seeming to be aware of the actress now sprawled in her seat. "Hughy. How are you?"

"Fine, Jake. I think Siobhan's too tired to go out somewhere to eat. I thought I would order in."

"Don't bother. I've already ordered from Lin Tang's. It should be here any moment. Would you mind if Siobhan and I used your office?"

Hughy shook his head, a half-irritated smile on his face, a shrugging look at Siobhan signaling defeat.

"Excuse me," Jake looked around at the group near the doors. "I think that may be our lunch now. I'll just direct them to your office." His hard smile moved over Siobhan. "You'll come along in a moment, won't you?" He left without waiting for her answer.

"Must that man steamroller everyone?" Siobhan's hands clenched and unclenched on her chair arms.

"He's been like that since I first knew him when we were at Princeton together. Even then I used to wonder why he didn't slow down and enjoy some of the perks of being rich." Hughy looked down at her for a moment, his smile fleeting.

"Join us for lunch," she begged shamelessly.

Hughy sighed. "The pleading in those violet eyes almost convinces me, but it wouldn't do any good, love. He'd just ask me to leave."

"Then I'm not going to eat with him," Siobhan announced, flouncing into the powder room marked Ladies and making up her mind to order a salad from the deli and an apple for dessert.

She came out of the bathroom section of the rest room feeling refreshed and determined. Jake was standing there. "What are you doing here?" she shrieked. "You can't come in here! Didn't you read the sign Ladies? Get out!" Siobhan breathed brimstone.

"I'll go, but you're coming with me." Jake pushed away from the wall with a thrust of those wide shoulders and stared at her.

"Someone is going to push you out a window," Siobhan fumed, pulling at his fingers as they closed on her arm.

He led her from the rest room into a small knot of people that included Hughy, waiting outside, all of them staring at the door. People scattered as Jake swept his glance over them. All but Hughy, who stared back.

"Will you stop acting like Attila the Hun?" Hughy looked at his friend with distaste. "Siobhan has enough on her mind without worrying about you coming at her like a tank."

"Make up your mind, friend. Either I'm a tank or a Hun." Jake kept walking, his hold on Siobhan not loosening.

"He's both," she gritted through clamped jaws.

Jake stopped in front of Hughy's office door, the gold lettering proudly proclaiming the status of Producer. "I will have her back in plenty of time for wardrobe. So if you will excuse us . . ." Jake gave his friend a salute and pushed Siobhan through the door in front of him.

"I would have preferred to eat with Hughy." She turned to face him, rubbing her upper arm where he had gripped it. "And I don't like caveman tactics," she glared at him.

To her surprise, he threw back his head and laughed. "Do you know you look like Little Lord Fauntleroy in that outfit?"

She looked down at her short skirt and flat heels, then up at him, cursing the flood of color rising in her face. "For your information, this outfit is considered very stylish."

He shook his head, dimples at the side of his mouth in evidence as he chuckled. "Don't get me wrong. I think you look adorable. But it is not an outfit for the sexpot Raine on 'Day By Day.'"

She tried to smother the smile that pulled at her mouth. "That's true. Raine would never be caught dead in such an outfit."

Jake walked closer to her, lifting the pristine white collar of the dress. "You still look very sexy. I have a feeling that you'd look that way in coveralls."

Siobhan stared up at him, feeling the melting-wax sensation in her legs that always happened when she was close to James Kendall Deerfield. "I think I should eat now," she squeaked.

"Right." Jake took her arm and led her over to Hughy's desk, which had been swept clean of papers.

Siobhan winced as she thought what long hours Hughy would spend looking for things in the jumbled pile that Jake had dumped onto the couch.

Jake lay out the food in the paper cartons on a white spread covering the oak desk.

"Linen too?" Her salivary glands began to activate as she saw the array of salads, vegetables and chicken that he grouped there.

They munched in silence, interspersing the food with sips of hot herbal tea.

Siobhan glanced at him from time to time and always found him watching her, his expression amused and ironic.

"Don't chew your lip that way. Let me. . . ." He lifted her out of her chair and onto his lap before she could do more than gulp. He held her tight to him when she tried to wriggle free. "Darling, if you do that, we'll be on Hughy's couch doing more than cuddling." He grinned when she went rock-still, his mouth taking small sucking bites of her lips. "You taste better than Chinese food," he whispered into her ear.

"I think Lin Tang would be affronted."

"We won't tell him."

"Lunch hour is up," Siobhan reminded him weakly.

"Have dinner with me tonight." Jake nuzzled her neck, the harshness of his breathing telling her that he was almost losing control, just as she was.

"I'll see." Her eyelids felt like lead. Speaking had become a chore.

"Tell me now you'll have dinner with me, or I'll keep you on my lap all day."

Her eyes snapped open. "You wouldn't!"

He shrugged and gave her a twisted smile, one finger moving, gently abrasive, down her nose. "Wanna put it to the test?"

She tried to break from the steel aura of those blue-black eyes, then shook her head in defeat.

"Does that mean you will have dinner with me?"

She nodded.

"Good." He swung her from his lap to her feet, steadying her by clasping her waist as he too rose from the chair. He kissed her nose. "Time to get to work. I'll pick you up here at five."

"Six," Siobhan bleated, wondering if there was a flight to Hong Kong at five.

"I'll be here." He lifted her close to his body, his mouth moving over hers until her lips parted. When his tongue touched hers, memory was like electricity, slicing downward into her body and reminding each atom of Siobhan Ryan-Vona Butler how totally his she had once been.

She pulled free and looked up at him, knowing that to arm herself against him, she would need space, time and cannons of her own.

"Tonight, darling." Jake let his hand slide from her waist to her backside, rubbing and patting there, before he turned her in his arms, walked her to the door and opened it. He kissed her neck, gently squeezed her derriere and released her.

Siobhan remained unmoving even when she heard the door close behind her. Her mind was already taking her away, finding a hideout, a deep dark cave, a bottomless well.

The stares of the others in the cast did not bother her when she returned to the studio. She was numb to everything but thoughts of escape.

At a short break in the afternoon, Hughy approached her.

"How do you feel about playing this torrid love scene with Breck Darrow?" His eyes scrutinized her.

"Am I correct in thinking that we have enough in the can for me to get away for a while?" Siobhan's words were forced past frozen lips.

Hughy was silent several seconds. "He got to you."

"Yes, he got to me. And he plans on getting to me

more. And I don't have enough ammunition to tell him to go to hell," she muttered.

"There's always the movie, 'Bare Facts.' Zenith still wants you for that, and I have an interest in Zenith, but Jake does not..." Hughy mused, keeping one eye on Del Krantz, who was watching them impatiently. "I have an idea. I'll talk to you about it over dinner."

"That Svengali is taking me to dinner."

Hughy exhaled, shaking his head. "He's a hard man to beat, is our Jake." All at once he snapped his fingers. "There was a telephone call for you, very important, someone named Maura."

She jerked erect. "Maura? My sister? It can't be. She's with my mother in Australia."

"Siobhan, for God's sake...we're losing time here..." Del Krantz called to her, his mouth worrying a dead cigar. Del had quit smoking cigars but he kept un-lit ones around to put in his mouth when he was agitated.

"Coming, coming," Siobhan looked harried as she stared at Hughy. "Call the number will you, Hughy? Find out if it is my sister, okay?"

"Siobhan," Del snarled.

THE AFTERNOON was long and arduous, but the love scene played without a hitch. Siobhan was so concerned about her sister and Jake that she played the coldhearted Raine with aplomb, putting the hero through a torrid love-play so that she could have control over him.

It was the last scene of the day and much of the set was cleared because there was a semi-nude scene in which she would be naked from the waist up, and though the glimpse of her breasts on camera would be more implied than actual, it called for realism.

When they were done, Breck Darrow helped her on with her robe. "You might be a bit too slim, darling, but you have great breasts," he breathed, kissing her cheek.

Siobhan stared at him, bored amusement in her voice. "Thanks, Breck, but you can cool your jets now. The heavy breathing segment is over."

"You can't blame a guy for trying." He gave her a friendly grin.

Then an arm came out and pushed Darrow in the chest, a voice growling "Get out of here!" Both Siobhan and Breck stared open-mouthed at Jake.

"Jake," Siobhan gasped, holding her wrap closed with one hand.

He turned to her as Breck melted away. "Tie that damn thing and get to your dressing room."

She was about to tell him to get lost, when Hughy grabbed her arm, turned her and marched her to the dressing room. "Wait a minute. I want to tell that cretin exactly what I think of him," she fumed.

"Better you should make love to the volcano Mauna Loa when it's in full spate than approach Jake when he's in a temper."

"What was he trying to prove?" She faced Hughy, arms akimbo.

"Never mind. Look, I called that number and Maura *was* your sister," Hughy reported as he held up a hand to forestall her questions. "And it's not only Maura, but your brother Lance as well. They'll be coming to stay with you after a visit to San Francisco."

"With Emma Deland," Siobhan murmured absently. "She's a cousin of my mother's." Her body felt like a rag doll. "I can't believe they've come all the way from Australia."

"It seems the Butler young 'uns want to seek their fortunes in New York," Hughy grinned at her.

"But what about school?"

"Maura said to remind you that she is nine months younger than you." Hughy was laughing now.

Openmouthed, she nodded. "That's true, but Lance is only eighteen. He's definitely going to school." Siobhan pushed her fingers into her temples and grimaced. "What timing! Just when I want to skip the country, I'll have to wait for them to arrive. What will I do in the meantime?"

Hughy shrugged. "That is a problem. You'll just have to tough out this week. But once they arrive. . ." Hughy looked smug, then he started to pace. "Do you remember where Jake and I stayed when we first met you?"

She felt a rush of blood up her neck. "Yes. It was Jake's home. You called it—" Siobhan snapped her fingers, trying to remember.

"Deerfield Hall. It's a great old barn of a place on about fifty acres of land—secluded, private, very nice."

"Hughy!" his friend pleaded. "What are you saying?"

"I'm saying that I asked Jake to let me use Deerfield Hall to do the revisions on that book I'm writing and he said yes. So if I leave here in, say, a week, with you, your brother and sister to stay for two weeks at Deerfield Hall, that will get you away."

"Jake wouldn't have to know?" Siobhan whispered, beginning to sniff rescue in the air.

"Siobhan," Jake's voice, coming through the door, penetrated her confusion. "Are you dressing?"

"Yes," she called, her hands hanging loose at her sides. She felt as though she had just been invited to a hanging, formal dress required.

"Think about it," Hughy hissed to her. She nodded.

Hughy grabbed the pin-striped, man-tailored suit in mauve silk. The faint stripe was the violet color of her eyes, matching the frilly silk blouse. Handing it to her, he urged her to dress.

"Hughy! Are you in there?" Jake growled.

"Coming out." Hughy rolled his eyes and drew the edge of his hand across his throat. He left the room, pulling the door shut behind him.

Siobhan heard the muted roar of Jake's voice as he castigated Hughy for remaining in her dressing room far too long.

She rose from her dressing table, twitching at the slender-legged trousers that hit just below her ankle bone, the plain black low-heeled pump looking more dashing than ordinary. She had twisted her hair in a knot on the left side of her head, wearing amethyst buttons in her ears, an amethyst pinkie ring and a gold watch and chain stretched across the vest.

She opened her door and stood there as the two men turned to gaze at her.

"You look like a silky George Sand," Jake drawled. "If you were trying to look unisex, darling, you failed miserably. Good night, Hughy." Jake reached for her, hardly giving her time to say good-night to anyone, let alone Hughy, who winked and nodded to her.

"Why did he do that?" Jake said, his voice casual, as they rode the elevator to the underground garage.

"What are you talking about?" She gazed up at him.

"Hughy winked at you." The words were bullets fired around the square cage of the elevator.

"He always does that when he says goodbye. We're good friends." Siobhan kept her eyes on him, even though her entire insides had liquified and were seeping from her pores.

"That's obvious. It's also obvious that you are not sexually involved with each other." Jake stood close, his body bent toward her. "No answer to that?"

"There is no answer to that." She was stiff with anger. "My personal life and who I may or may not share it with is none of your business, Mr. Deerfield."

"So angry—so independent. *Now* you don't see how it is with us, but you will."

The elevator doors opened into the dankness of the underground garage and rather than trade words with him, she pressed her lips tight and marched forward.

"This way, my darling."

"I am not your darling."

"Yes, you are."

The ride to Danilo's took less than half an hour, but Siobhan didn't break the silence. Instead she listened to the taped music, trying to forget the man next to her. *That's like climbing Mount Washington in roller skates,* she fumed.

Danilo's was jumping. The club side had a dance band and the restaurant side looked filled to capacity.

"I hope you like Italian food," Jake breathed in her ear.

"I do. In fact, I think I shall have calamari," Siobhan announced.

"I like squid, too. We can have that and maybe fried burdocks."

"Fine." They followed the waiter who escorted them to a rather secluded table, with a latticed screen fronted by potted plants affording them privacy.

After she'd looked at the varied items on the menu, her mouth was watering, and she wished that she could have ordered the canneloni rather than the squid but she knew she would never tell Jake that.

When he took the menu from her and ordered in Italian for both of them, she was dumbfounded and didn't find her voice until the wine steward had left with their order. "Did it never occur to you that I might like to order my own dinner?"

"It did, but since I know Danilo's chef, I ordered for both of us. Don't worry, there will be squid and burdocks included." He slid around the bench seat until they were sitting shoulder to shoulder. "When you see what is brought, you won't be angry with me any more."

"I'm not angry with you, Mr. Deerfield. I'm bloody furious." She looked up at him, inhaling deeply.

"Do you know when you do that even through the vest and blouse your breasts swell beautifully." He leaned closer. "And stop calling me Mr. Deerfield." His tongue came out to touch her ear. "Tell me why you did that scene topless."

"The script called for it." Siobhan felt a shudder go through her.

"I saw it—and I hated that damned Darrow for seeing you like that."

She looked up, distracted from her anger. "Breck? He's harmless." Siobhan smiled, thinking of the man she had worked with for so many months.

"Is he? I don't think so." Jake shifted so he was almost facing her, forcing her against the leather banquette.

"I feel like peanut butter between two slices of bread." She could see the tiny lines that rayed out from his eyes, the dots of gold in the dark blue of the iris. "Could you give me a little more room?"

"No. I'm always going to hold you, keep you close to me." Jake pronounced it like a death sentence.

"No doubt we'll spill food on each other."

His smile was slow, like a first star appearing in a summer sky. "You have so much spirit, you should have been two women. I once knew—" Jake paused and flicked her cheek with his finger.

"What were you going to say?"

"Nothing." He looked at each feature of her heart-shaped face. "I love your nose. Straight, but with character. And your mouth...."

"Tell me what you were going to say a moment ago."

"Do you always interrupt a man when he's making love to you?"

"Oh? Is that what you're doing?" Siobhan grinned at him, making his lazy smile disappear at once. She stared at him when she saw him swallow once, twice. "What is it?"

"I would like you to do that for me at least once a day—smile like that."

Bereft of words, she watched that face come closer, her eyes closing of their own volition.

"Your antipasto, sir. Shall I serve it or—"

"We'll serve ourselves," Jake snapped.

The man disappeared.

"You were a little hard on him, weren't you?" Siobhan offered tentatively.

"Not hard enough." Jake turned to face the monstrous platter of cold vegetables, anchovies and rolled meat, taking the tongs himself and placing choice pieces on Siobhan's plate.

"No anchovies, please," she told him.

He smiled at her. "Surprise! Something you don't like."

"Not true. I like anchovies...but not in a salad...or pizza. I like them alone with lemon juice," she assured him.

"Woman, you delight me." Jake fed her from his fork and gestured that she should do the same.

"I thought it was only the Greeks—" She stumbled into silence.

"—that fed their betrothed from their plates. True. Would you like to be my . . . woman . . . so that I could feed you from my plate all the time?"

Would you like to be my woman! Indeed! "I'm aware of the great *honor* you wish to confer on me." She hoped that all her teeth were showing in the smile she turned on him. "But—I must decline."

He looked down at her. "Did you expect an offer of marriage?"

"I expect nothing from you." She fought to keep her tone neutral.

"I see."

Her head whipped up so that she was staring into those eyes again. "I hope you do. I should hate to have to repeat myself."

Those star-sapphire eyes became blue fire. "Back off, Siobhan. You're becoming tiresome."

"Am I?" Her voice was low as she pushed around the bench seat. "Excuse me, I'm going to the powder room." She flashed him a plastic smile, so very tempted to take the Baked Alaska flambé from a passing cart and dump it in his lap.

Passing the door marked Ladies, then past the cloak room, her cold smile barely touched the doorman as she ordered a cab.

The ride back to her apartment was a blur. The red mist in front of her eyes prevented Siobhan from seeing the myriad lights of Manhattan or hearing the droning monologue of the driver.

She paid him and entered the foyer with a key, again

pushing her key into the elevator and riding it up to her floor.

The phone was ringing as she entered the apartment. She stared at it for a few moments, goose bumps coating her skin. "Go to hell, Jake Deerfield."

When the jangling stopped, she breathed a sigh of relief. She went into her bedroom and stripped the clothes from her body, then went into the bathroom.

She stood under the full blast of the shower for long minutes, letting the stinging hot water take some of the numbness away.

She was hanging up her clothes, her hair turbaned in a towel, when the doorbell started ringing. What would Hughy want at this time of night? And it must be Hughy, she reasoned, leaving the bedroom. Who else, with a key for the elevator, would be at her door at—she glanced at her watch—five minutes to midnight.

Yawning, she stood in front of the door, one eye at the peephole, so she could look out into the corridor.

Damn! Jake was there and he was looking right at the peephole. She was about to creep away from the door and hide out in her bedroom, but when she turned, her thigh struck the hall table, rattling it.

"Siobhan. Open this—or I'll open it the hard way." Jake's sibilant hiss penetrated the steel door.

She slowly opened the door with the chain on. "How did you get a key for the elevator?"

"From the super. He's known me since Hughy and I were in school."

"Oh. I'm tired."

"I want to talk to you." His graven face changed, tension skittering across its surface. He rubbed one hand through his hair. "Siobhan, please."

She opened the door wide and he stepped through to walk into the lounge, then turned to face her.

"Why did you leave Danilo's?" He watched her, hands hanging loose at his side.

She swallowed. "We don't get along, Mr. Deerfield."

"Call me Jake, Siobhan." His eyes penetrated her. "We had a bad start, and it was my fault. I can't explain why, but I'd like to start again."

Siobhan stared at him, seeing hunger there. She looked away from him. "Can I offer you—"

He reached out his hand to her, palm upward. "I don't need anything. I want to talk to you."

She walked toward him as though a silken pulley were reeling her to him. She put her hand in his, then looked down at their entwined fingers. When she looked up again, it didn't surprise her to see his head coming down to hers.

His lips were hesitant, testing, until he felt her body sway into his. Then his mouth hardened, savored, took. His arms lifted her clear of the floor, his mouth still seeking and tasting hers.

When his tongue touched hers, she again felt the long-ago fire that she had tamped down in her mind when she had dreamed of Jake Deerfield. Flaring at once, it ignited both of them.

He lifted his head for a moment and stared down at her, his breathing shallow. "Siobhan, you're a witch with those eyes. You make me remember—and I want to forget."

She tried to pull back from him, free herself, but his arms tightened. "You said you wanted to talk," she offered, to still the shudder that coursed through her.

"You aren't cold, are you, love? I know that dressing gown is pretty thin." Jake slurred his words as his fingers feathered up and down her back, touching each bone and muscle there.

"No. I'm not cold." She told herself to push away from him, but when he led her to the couch and drew her down beside him, she didn't resist.

He reached up and pulled at the knot in his tie, jerking it loose. "Fighting with you is the last thing I want," Jake said. "I'd much rather make love to you." His brooding blue stare covered her like midnight-black satin. He reached up and touched her lips. "It's too soon for you, I know, but I want to get to know you. I want you to get to know me." He looked down at his hands hanging between his knees, then back at her. "I want a future with you, Siobhan."

Siobhan licked her lips. "I know your reputation, your women—"

"And you don't want that." Jake finished. He inhaled. "I don't know what I want with you, Siobhan—or what you want with me. But I do know I don't want to lose you, or what we have between us."

She watched that strong face come toward hers. Her hand reached up to cup his jaw. "Jake," she breathed.

"Yes, darling."

White flame burned through her, taking away her protest, melting it and fusing her to him. She could feel his gasps in her mouth as though he were breathing for both of them.

When he swung her onto his lap, his hand moving to her thigh, her anguished "no" was buried in her throat.

His hand traveled up her bare leg, pushing aside her dressing gown.

"No!" she gasped. "No!" Blood filled her veins until she thought they would pop through her skin. Every nerve in her body pulsated with delight.

"Easy, love." Jake spoke to her, but his eyes were on her body, almost completely uncovered to his gaze. "You're so beautiful." His brow furrowed. "Those eyes...."

She pushed back from him, sat up and rolled from his lap, staggering to her feet. "No. You must leave. I'm tired." Siobhan sparred for time.

Jake rose to his feet and caught her to him. "Don't look like that. You don't have to fear me." He kissed the damp tendrils clinging to her forehead. "What we have between us is very special, Siobhan with the beautiful name. Fast or slow, how ever long it takes, I want to teach you that." His mouth came down, softly rubbing hers. "Good night, my darling." He left so fast that she was still standing next to the couch, her mouth open, her hands hanging limply at her sides.

She rushed into bed, keeping her mind as blank as she could, not wanting to think of Jake. Sleep came like a slowly booming drum, blocking all sound, all thought, all fear.

FOR THE rest of the week, the days were filled with work and phone calls from Maura and Lance to say they were on the way. The nights were filled with Jake.

Each night he picked her up from work and took her to dinner. One evening they went dancing. Then they would come back to her apartment, where he would make slow, sensuous love to her, always stopping before culmination. Her body fevered for him and for his love.

She could sense his iron control was cracking even as hers was. She had no doubt that they would fully make love one evening soon.

"Hughy," Siobhan begged one night in a rare moment

alone with her friend. "Maura and Lance are coming tomorrow, on the early flight. You'll pick them up, won't you? Then we'll go away the next day, okay?"

Hughy put an arm around her. "It's all set. I'll take them to my apartment. You leave the studio and—"

"And go out with Jake," she moaned, biting her bottom lip.

"He isn't a monster, sweetie. Don't worry."

She smiled weakly and nodded. The rest of the day was hectic and she was able to put Jake out of her mind.

When he picked her up that evening she was wearing a black silk suit with a violet blouse.

They went to Dominie's to dance after dining, and Siobhan could feel the tiny hairs on her body standing straight out. She felt welded to Jake by an erotic charge as they stepped and moved in slow rhythm.

She noted the smile of awareness on Dominie's face when they said good-night, but she was in such a haze of love that she barely responded.

When they entered her apartment, Siobhan turned to him, her face lifted, her arms reaching up to him as he leaned down to kiss her.

It seemed right when he lifted her and carried her into the bedroom and lay down beside her on the bed. Clothes were discarded with careless dispatch as each looked hungrily at the other. In minutes they were naked, lips to lips, face to face, form to form on the crisp sheets.

Her mouth opened on his, as though all the deep, embedded wishes in her psyche were surfacing through her skin. He was all the man and held all the love that Siobhan had dreamed of, and she gave herself to him gladly, not listening to the voice deep inside her that told her she could never keep him.

They held, tasted and sucked, letting their feelings crackle between them.

"Tall—but so tiny—but not here . . ." Jake's rasping voice enveloped her in passion, lifting her out of herself so that she began caressing him, touching him, her hands gliding down his body, taking hold of him intimately, delighting when he groaned.

When his fingers probed and teased her body, Siobhan melted like a candle. Her tongue entered his mouth, seeking and finding his teeth, the roof of his mouth, wanting to taste all of him as her body writhed at his side.

She felt his mouth circle down her body, then enter where his hand had been. She heard herself cry out, then she was gasping with pleasure as Jake swung her under him and entered her with a powerful gentleness. The torrid rhythm spun them away, binding them to one another.

I love you, Jake, I love you, she called out in her mind.

He didn't leave until early morning, and even then he was reluctant, seeming unable to get enough of her.

When he was gone, she stood in the foyer, tears coursing down her cheeks. "It's too late, too late. I love him and he'll swallow me whole."

Still shuddering, she dialed Hughy's number.

"Hey, it's six in the morning. The flight doesn't arrive. . . . Are you crying? What is it?"

"We have to go today . . ." she whispered, her voice hoarse.

Hughy was silent for a long moment. "Today it is, then. Call Del and tell him you're taking a holiday."

She went with Hughy to the airport and wept over her sister and brother—all three of them talking at the same time.

Hughy had to explain what they were going to do and why they were going to Deerfield Hall. He outlined their plans as they headed back to Siobhan's apartment to pick up her things.

She braided her hair in one long plait, then pinned it in a circle to the back of her head, tying a kerchief over the whole thing.

It took her a long time to compose a note to the super which would not give away where she was. HOLD ALL MAIL, she wrote, I WILL CALL PERIODICALLY TO CHECK ON WHAT HAS COME THROUGH.

Loading her bags was not too difficult, because Lance was there to help, but still they had to strap some of the cases on top of the roomy Mercedes.

They drove away from Manhattan with frequent glances from Hughy and Siobhan out the rear window of the car.

"Is Jake a gangster or what?" Maura raised her eyebrows as she sat in the back seat, smiling at Hughy when he looked at her in the rearview mirror. "He sounds sexy." Her smile widened at Hughy.

"Someone will fit him with cement shoes one day." Siobhan pronounced in doomsday tones.

Hughy gave a hard laugh. "More likely it would be Jake taking care of the person who tried to put them on him. He is one tough cookie and neither Groton nor Princeton nor dancing lessons and deportment at Madame Solane's ever changed that."

"He took dancing?" Siobhan breathed.

"And deportment," Hughy chuckled, shaking his head. "Still, I always considered him a good friend— until now." Hughy frowned at the rearview mirror, then his face softened to a smile as he looked at Maura again.

"I'm questioning your own intentions in that area,"

Siobhan drawled, alluding to his interest in her sister.

Hughy's knuckles whitened on the wheel, and Siobhan leaned over and patted his knee. "Don't you know that I consider you one mellow man for any woman."

Hughy smiled at her, then snapped his fingers as a thought struck him. "Maura, you and Lance should get used to calling Vona Siobhan. That's her professional name. And it wouldn't be good for Jake to hear you call your sister Vona."

"Why not?" Lance quizzed. "Or is it a deep, dark secret?"

"For now it is." Siobhan grinned at him, hoping her flip-flopping stomach didn't show in her smile. There was no telling what Jake would do if he found her living with Hughy at Deerfield Hall. And with a brother and sister as well!

3

THE FIRST DAYS at Deerfield Hall were tense ones for Siobhan, but little by little she began to relax and enjoy the rich and varied environment.

The third afternoon, Maura, who had been helping Hughy with his editing, convinced her sister and him to come down to the stables and go riding with her and Lance.

Siobhan was shaken to her shoes. Though her brother and sister were totally at ease with the equine inhabitants of the stable, she had never had the earthy tuition in riding that they had enjoyed, living on a ranch in Australia. Of course, Hughy, who had been taught to ride at an early age, was quite proficient.

"Don't be silly, Vona—I mean, Siobhan. That mare is nothing but a lap dog." Lance was amused and a little disgusted as his sister took a death grip on the reins.

"It's so high!" she croaked, opening one eye.

"Fourteen hands!" Lance was openly scathing. "It's no higher than a bike."

"Liar," Siobhan muttered, afraid of making too much noise in the company of four such large creatures. She blinked every time Lance's horse snorted and reared, even though her brother assured her that the animal was only fresh and ready to go.

"He's just showing his oats, miss. Not an ounce of malice is there, in old Jupiter." Stableman Amos White moved over to the neck of Siobhan's horse. "And this here Nancy—why, she's a perfect lady. Carry ya nice as ya please."

"Lovely," she bleated, watching as Hughy and Lance brought their horses alongside hers and urged her to get moving.

For several outings, Maura, Hughy and Lance stayed with her, giving Siobhan instructions. But though Siobhan nodded and told them she understood, she was still never able to escape the fear that assailed her each time she mounted.

Finally one morning, she was able to convince Hughy and Lance not to wait for her, but instead to gallop across the flat open ground leading to the woods that bordered on the Hudson River.

"I'll stay with you," Maura promised.

"Stop being a martyr and go after them, Maura. I'll be fine. Don't worry. Nancy knows her way around the place."

Maura left, urging her horse into a jumping gallop, lying far over its neck.

Murmuring in wonderment, Siobhan nudged Nancy into a sedate walk along the drive. The horse minced down the gravel until she came to a well-worn path, on to which she turned, following it at a slow, rolling gait across the meadow. "You are a lady," her rider spoke in low tones, "just as Amos said you were." She patted the glossy neck of the bay mare and began to think that it wouldn't be too bad going this distance after the boredom of riding around the paddock.

Around her, the rolling pastureland was riotous with spring. Forsythia was still in bloom, but fading a bit. Everywhere underfoot there were dying, but still colorful, crocuses and budding daffodils. "A giant mystical gardener planted this meadow and hillside just for us, Nancy."

The mare nickered softly and kept on her plodding way. They had almost crossed the entire meadow when Siobhan felt a soreness in her inner legs, at the calf and thigh. She shifted her weight on the horse and Nancy sped up her walk to a trot, jiggling her rider off balance, so that she gripped the horse's mane as well as the reins. Nancy slowed to a stop.

"Thank you for stopping, Nancy," Siobhan panted. Then she gripped the horse's mane again when the mare began the semi-steep climb up the path and out of the meadow. "Where are we going, Nancy? Isn't it time we went back? You can have your oats and I can have a hot bath. Oooooh, my legs are sore." She tried several times to turn the horse in the direction they had come, but Nancy had a mind of her own.

"There she is!"

The shout came from behind Siobhan so she didn't turn around, for fear of falling right off the horse.

Horses were everywhere all at once. Lance charged ahead of her on the path, his horse rearing, making Siobhan blink. Nancy didn't seem to be impressed.

"Where have you been?" Lance's eyes sparkled as he swung down from the horse and walked back to his sister's side. "We were looking for you."

"In all the wrong places, no doubt." She patted Nancy. "Nancy didn't want to go home right away. She was taking me for a ride."

"She was taking you right back to the stable," Hughy laughed. "That old girl knows all the shortcuts back to the feed bin."

Siobhan smiled as she tried to turn and look at Hughy. The movement caused her legs to hurt even more. "I think I'll be glad to get back and get off Nancy... even though I must say she is a lady."

Maura rode ahead down the ridge path that overlooked the meadow, Lance walking his horse next to Siobhan.

"You aren't angry that we're here with you, are you, sis?"

Siobhan stopped Nancy again, trying not to groan at the increased chafing and muscle discomfort she was feeling. "Lance, all of us were close, you know that. When I was left here at nineteen to finish school, I thought I'd die of loneliness." She reached out for her brother's hand. "Having you and Maura here with me is a bonus I never looked for, and I'm delighted."

Lance nodded his head in a jerky way. "Thanks, sis. That's the way Maura and me and the rest of us feel about you." He grinned as he spurred his horse. "Now if only we didn't have to worry about Mr. Deerfield...." Lance's voice floated out behind him.

"And why did you have to mention his name?" Siobhan winced. "Aren't I in enough pain without putting me on the rack?" Nancy nickered when her rider spoke.

The path took a downward snakelike turn and the push of her body forward in the saddle had her groaning. Through the trees, she saw the outlines of the barns and stables and wondered how she would ever make it that far.

Hughy and Maura were already rubbing down their horses when Nancy crossed the stableyard. Lance, coming out of the barn, waved to his sister.

"Shall I help you down?" Lance made cooing sounds to the mare as he approached her.

Hughy looked up from what he was doing and nodded to a hovering groom to take his horse. "I think we may have to peel her from that saddle."

Siobhan glared at the chuckling Hughy, almost falling into his arms. Both Lance and Hughy held her erect, her rubbery legs refusing to do the job. "Stop braying and help me into the house."

"You two are awful. Here, Siobhan, lean on me." Maura put her arm around her sister's waist.

"We'll take her, Maur." Lance was still laughing as he pushed Maura to one side.

"Sadists." Siobhan gritted her teeth as they led her through the kitchen entrance and up some back stairs.

The men left her in Maura's hands at the bedroom door.

"Isn't it super that Mr. Deerfield has a hot tub in his own private apartments?" Maura glowed. "You could go in there instead of into a regular tub. Not that this bathroom between our rooms isn't great! It is. I've never seen one so big."

Siobhan stared at her younger sister as she struggled to undress. "Are you sure he has a hot tub?"

"Hughy showed it to me." Maura had a smug glitter in her eye.

"You like him? Hughy, I mean?" Siobhan wrapped a silk dressing gown around herself.

"He's a cupcake." Maura frowned as her sister limped toward the door. "Where are you going?"

"To use Jake's hot tub. Why should I risk spending the night in agony when I can soak and whirl away my aches?" She braced herself against the door frame and looked back at Maura. "Coming?"

Mouth agape, Maura moved toward her sister. "Hughy said we were not to go into his apartments."

"Hughy can pound salt," Siobhan glowered. "He

thinks it's so funny for me to be twisted like a pretzel after riding a horse! Forget it—I'm going to use that hot tub."

Maura's stare melted into a mischievous grin and nodded. "Let's do it. The old goat will never know."

Siobhan grinned at the idea of the virile, powerful body and hard-planed face of Jake Deerfield being called an old goat. *No way*, she thought.

Jake's suite was in another wing, and for a moment, when Maura approached the door leading to that wing, Siobhan had a sinking feeling that it might be locked.

When Maura turned the handle and pushed open the door, Siobhan sagged with relief. At least she wouldn't have to make her way back through the labyrinth of corridors without a soothing session in the hot tub.

"Isn't it beautiful in here, Vona?" Maura spoke in hushed tones as they passed through a smaller version of the library downstairs, then a well-appointed lounge that was larger than her whole apartment, and finally through an even larger bedroom with a huge round bed, the color scheme throughout being cream and midnight-blue.

Like his eyes, Siobhan thought, trying to push the image of them from her mind.

"Did you ever see so much silk and satin?" Maura was still whispering. "And look at that bed! A regular passion pit, it is." Maura's accent was pure Australian as she looked in awe around her.

"Only a decadent man would have a deep-blue silk bedspread like that," Siobhan muttered, remembering that the rooms had been in brown and orange when she had been here last. How she wanted to forget! Not even Hughy knew.

She hobbled to the bathroom that was tiled in Mexi-

can *azuelos*, mostly in cream, interspersed with deeper
blue. There had not been a hot tub when she had been
here before. But she wasn't a naive twenty-two-year-old
now either...

"Vona, why are you squeezing the soap that way?
You've dug your nails almost through it." Maura
frowned at the subtly perfumed soap and didn't see the
color rise in Siobhan's face.

"Just daydreaming, I guess." She looked at her younger sister, feeling more agitated than she'd expected at being in Jake's quarters. "Ah, why don't you go down and
join Hughy and Lance, and keep them from coming upstairs and finding that I'm in this room." All at once, she
was desperate for privacy, so that she might get hold of
herself and talk her stupid memory out of dredging up
old news. Jake Deerfield! Old news!

"All right," Maura saluted, grinning. "I'll just get the
two of them talking about themselves. That should keep
them busy."

When her sister left, Siobhan switched the tempera-
ture higher, then leaned against the wall recalling so
many things that moved through her mind.

What would Jake say if he could see her now? They
had showered together, years ago, after they made love
in his bedroom. He had held her and washed her and
caressed her in the shower, the tight squeeze in the small
cubicle sheer heaven to her.

She stared into space, hearing her own laughter when
Jake had dried her, then carried her back to the bedroom, both naked, unable to keep their hands off each
other.

Siobhan closed her eyes, but she couldn't blot out
how she had responded to him then. She had wanted
him so much. "Fool," she muttered. She gnashed her

teeth as she recalled herself writhing beneath him, as she heard herself call out, "I love you, I love you." Had she said it out loud? She splashed water in her eyes as she sat up suddenly, one hand pressed to her mouth.

Again Jake sprang into her mind.

He had moved restlessly over her, both their bodies damp from the shower, his fully aroused. He had begun to kiss the curves of her knees and her elbows. He kissed her wrists, her arms, then her toes, her feet, all the way up her legs, his mouth intimate on her body, finally joining her in the ultimate intimacy.

"No, no, no, no . . ." she groaned, her eyes open, but still unable to blank out the picture of the two fused figures from her memory.

She lowered herself into the steaming, swirling water, letting the frothing liquid soothe and massage her aching muscles. "Why did I come here? Why didn't I know that my memories would be sharper here, that I wouldn't be able to stop thinking about how it was. Damn him for coming back into my life."

She tried to think of flowers, of books she had read, of the expanded role she would be playing on television next season.

"Hughy said I could do that movie for television that Zenith is getting ready," Siobhan muttered, almost asleep as the water tossed her gently in the tub.

She felt water up her nose and awoke with a jerk, coughing. *Lord, how long have I been in this tub? If I don't get out of here, Hughy or Lance will find that I've been in Jake's apartment,* she chastised herself, trying to stifle the yawns that came one upon the other. As she pulled herself out of the tub, deciding she would take her cool-down shower in her own quarters, she wrapped one of the huge bath sheets, stacked in the bathroom, around her body, hefted her robe and left Jake's apartment.

Dinner that night was a little uncomfortable for her. Despite the relaxing effects of the hot tub, she still had aches and pains. Even for the short duration of the dinner, she found sitting uncomfortable.

When the others sat around drinking coffee after dinner Siobhan decided that she had had enough and went to bed.

Aches and pains she had, but they still didn't keep her from sleeping. The clear, cool air and the exercise had affected her like a tranquilizer.

The next few days she worked with Hughy on his book, but found him restless, his eyes often going to the huge double doors leading from the library to the hall.

"Am I boring you?" She couldn't keep the amusement from her voice.

"Huh? Ah, no. Maura said she might stop by and give a hand...." Hughy glanced at her. "And you needn't chortle like some overstuffed hen. I'm just trying to be nice to your sister."

"You're succeeding." Siobhan's laugh was open.

"She's quite beautiful," Hughy stated, a muscle jumping in his cheek.

"I agree," she smiled at her friend.

"I asked her to go with me to a play the university players are putting on. Lance is coming with us." He reached into his pocket. "I was able to get four tickets."

Siobhan sighed and stretched her legs out in front of her. "Don't count on me, Hughy," she smiled, thinking that she would be able to enjoy the hot tub in Jake's suite without having to sneak there after the others had gone to bed. She hadn't even mentioned to Maura that she had been using the tub every evening before she went to bed. It was the only way she could keep from screaming at the bruising she was getting from horseback riding each day. She was sure that her body would never take to riding the way her sister's and brother's and Hughy's did.

They worked a little more than an hour before Maura joined them. Siobhan began to feel like a fifth wheel as Hughy and Maura conversed in a steady stream. It wasn't long before she excused herself.

"I think I'll take a walk around the grounds before dinner." Siobhan stood, watching the other two as they gazed into each other's eyes.

"A walk would do you good," Hughy agreed, his eyes leaving Maura for a millisecond.

"Thank you," Siobhan stated.

Maura looked up, a fatuous smile on her face. "You're welcome." Her gaze slid back to Hughy.

Siobhan did walk through the gardens, then she watched Lance jump his horse in the dressage corral that Amos said had been used when "the master" was a boy.

Amos had come to lean companionably on the fence beside Siobhan. He tapped his blackened pipe against his boot before tamping fresh tobacco into the bowl and lighting it. "He's a fine boy, that one, and he seems to be good at his books as well as with horses," Amos informed her.

She smiled at the grizzled man. "Has he been coming down to the barn and taking your time with questions?"

"Aye, and he asks many of them, he does." Amos almost smiled. "He thinks that I might know some of the answers."

"As I'm sure you do." Siobhan shook her head when Lance sailed over bales of hay that he had stacked. "I just hope he doesn't break his neck doing that." She watched her brother dismount from his horse.

Lance walked over to them leading the horse. "I'll just rub him down, then I'll come back to the house with you, sis. I wanted to tell you that I've decided to audit some classes at the university when we get back. When I start full-time in September, it will be a big help that I sat through some of the classes."

She nodded, proud of her tall, younger brother.

"I'll take him back to the stables with me and rub him down, Mr. Lance." Amos took the reins from Lance and led the horse away.

Siobhan pushed her hand through Lance's arm. "I really am glad that you and Maura came to me. I hadn't realized until I saw you both how homesick I was for family."

"It's great here. I wish we could live here." Lance grinned at her as they walked into the house to wash up for dinner.

The next day, Siobhan read the Zenith script while Maura worked with Hughy on his book and Lance helped Amos in the stable.

It took her a great deal of arguing that evening to convince Hughy and Maura and Lance that she wouldn't be going with them.

"I'd really like to go over the script again. I liked it . . ." she smiled at Hughy. "There's more to it on the second read—many things that I've missed the first time around—that are an integral part of the story. I want to know every nuance before I commit myself."

"I think Siobhan's made up her mind not to come." Maura studied her sister. Finally convinced the three of them left in a flurry of coats, forgotten purse, gloves and the squeal from Maura: "Lance, you promised that you'd wear a tie."

"I did. It's in my pocket. I'll put it on in the car."

Siobhan was laughing by the time they screeched down the drive in Hughy's Mercedes.

It was luxury in the extreme to settle down on the large sofa in the library, the fire that the housekeeper, Mrs. White, had started in the fireplace a comfort on the damp spring evening.

She had been reading for more than an hour when her aching shoulder began to interfere with her concentration.

Sighing, she rose to her feet and stretched, wincing when her sore shoulder muscle pulled. "Hot tub, here I come," she muttered to herself.

Taking the script with her, she checked the screen in front of the dying fire, turned down the lamp to a night light, then left the library and climbed the stairs to her room.

She undressed and donned her silky robe. Suddenly, Jake's image materialized in the mirror as she was removing her makeup. "Get thee behind me, Satan." She muttered at her reflection. "And that's what you are, James Kendall Deerfield. You are Lucifer himself, going through life taking women at your whim and whitewashing yourself by calling them tramps." She shuddered, the burning anger that she thought gone and forgotten erupting within her. "Not even Hughy knows that you picked me up from work that day, Jake—he doesn't know that you drove me out here to Deerfield Hall." She turned on the gold taps and the Jacuzzi switch. "I had put you away, Jake, in a dark corner of my mind, and now I'm back at Deerfield Hall and I find I can't bury that night any more." She squeezed the fluffy towel between her hands as she traversed the corridor back to her rooms to get the carryall with her shampoo and soap.

On her return to Jake's bath, she emptied her bag of toiletries onto the tile counter, placing the shampoo next to the shower cubicle. As long as no one was around, she could indulge herself by showering here, rather than running back to her own room.

She was floating lazily in the foaming water, letting the rhythm of the water massage away her aches, when another painful memory surfaced in her mind. That last day before she met Hughy in New York, before she said goodbye to New Paltz and joined her fortunes with Hughy's. Why? Why had she gone with him that day? He had insulted her. She didn't like him. He didn't like her. Why had he come to the diner at her quitting time that day? Why had she gone with him? His face was there, his mocking smile seeming magnified in the enclosed area.

Smoky images of my lost love, Siobhan thought, biting her lip, *because I did love him. In that short blinding moment, I did love him, but now I hate him,* she grated in her mind.

Lacerated feelings erupted in her mind as she saw Vona Butler, the girl who had dyed her hair a brassy red to look older, to fend off the unwelcome advances that were rife in the diner. She watched as Vona talked with Jake outside the diner in the early evening after the supper rush.

"I have to get to class," Vona explained.

"I'll pick you up after class. We'll go for a ride."

Siobhan could still remember how excitement had bloomed in her at the thought of going for a ride in Jake's Ferrari. She had nodded, then left him to run to class.

She alternated between elation and despair all through her class that night.

She finally convinced herself that he wouldn't show up at all, so it was no surprise to her when she left the university that evening and didn't see the Ferrari.

She was almost home when his car screeched up behind her and the passenger door was thrust open. "Get in. Sorry I'm late."

Vona wanted to tell him to go to hell. "It's late. I have studying to do."

Jake slammed the gears into neutral, pulled on the brake and came out of the car and around to her in one swift move. "Vona Butler, I was late because I was on the phone to New York. I promise that I won't keep you out late." He shrugged, taking hold of her upper arms. "Let me show you my home, Deerfield Hall. I'll make us something to eat, show you the place...." The velvet drawl pierced her armor, melting the argument she had had with herself in class about the callous person who had called her a sow's ear and whether such a person could change.

"Oh, has Hughy come back from New York?" Vona asked as he helped her into the car and closed the door on the passenger side.

"No, he hasn't," Jake slid behind the wheel and looked at her before he engaged the gears. "How did you know Hughy was in New York?"

Vona shrugged and looked out the window, not wanting to tell him that Hughy had promised to help her launch her career in acting, and that, as of tomorrow, she would be leaving New Paltz to try her luck in New York under Hughy's wing. "He must have mentioned it when I was serving him his food."

"Oh." Jake gazed at her for a long moment before driving the car through the town and out onto the darkened country roads.

Deerfield Hall was a shock to Vona. She had known that Jake must be rich by the car he drove, but she had not been prepared to see original Frederick Remingtons on the walls of his home.

"Is he a special favorite of yours?" Jake asked as he led her through the house on a guided tour, finishing in the kitchen where he made them a fruit and cheese board with a white wine accompaniment.

Jake touched her hair. "I would love to see the real color of your hair. What was it?"

"Ah, about the same," Vona lied, not wanting to explain to him why she had dyed her hair. It sounded too silly.

"Even with that funny-colored hair, Vona Butler, you are a cute cookie." Jake tightened his hold on her. "I felt you stiffen. You're angry that I made the comment about your hair. Aren't you?"

"No," Vona looked away from him.

His strong teeth nipped at her neck. "Yes, you are. I'm sorry that I hurt your feelings, but you wouldn't want me to tell you I liked you dyeing your hair. I don't." He kissed her, not a peck, but a deep, lasting, tongue-teasing kiss that made Vona's toes curl in her low-heeled shoes.

"Show me the rest of the house," Vona gasped, feeling her world turn upside down and around again. None of the boys she had dated had ever made her feel like melting wax, but Jake did that to her. She put her hands on his shoulders and pushed back from him.

Jake led her from room to room, suite to suite, his hand holding tightly to hers, his body bumping hers in gentle rhythm as they moved.

With each step, Vona could feel her control slipping. Jake, with every breath he inhaled, was pulling her close to him. Her blood was pumping with his.

He pushed open double doors. "This is the master wing of the house. Since my parents never come here anyway, I've taken that over for my own. Like it?"

Vona was hesitant when she entered the apartment, liking the orange and brown of the color scheme, but knowing that she wouldn't have chosen such a color combination for the rooms.

"What don't you like, Vona?"

"I do like it. It's just that—there are so many beautiful antiques in here, and they don't show as well with this color combination."

"Ah, yes, don't tell me. Waitressing is only a hobby. Your real job is as an interior designer."

Vona wheeled away from him and stalked from the room and down the hall. When she felt herself caught around the waist, she struggled, then fought him in earnest. She had promised herself long ago that she would let no one demean her, that if anyone ever struck at her in malice she would protect herself. She was proud of who she was, of who she sprang from—her father, her mother, her family—and no one could ever make small of that. "Take your stinking, money-grubbing hands off me," she shrieked, ready to fight until her last breath.

Jake's hands dropped from her at once.

They stood there, staring at each other, the only sound in the cavernous house their rasping breaths.

"I was out of line," Jake gasped.

"I want out of this house, away from you." Vona panted, her fists raised in front of her as though she would go at him again.

"Vona, listen to me—"

"I'm leaving," she shrilled at him, her body beginning to shake.

"I'm sorry. I didn't mean—I was wrong. Please, forgive me." Jake leaned over her and put his forehead on her clenched hands.

Shudders ran through her body as she stayed there unmoving, wanting to escape from him, but needing to be near him too. Vona was as sure as any street-wise girl could be that Jake presented a danger to her. Years of fending off men and taking care of herself, had taught her the danger signs. She recognized them all in Jake. Yet she wanted to stay with him, be with him, love him.

Her hands opened and her fingers began caressing his face instead of clawing it.

When he lifted his head to look at her, his mouth twisted. "Don't cry, Vona, don't cry." He leaned toward her, wiping away the tears that flowed in mascaraed streaks down her face.

"I don't want to make you cry. Nor do I want anyone ever to hurt you," Jake said, an awed twist to his voice, as though the words surprised him, as though he hadn't known what he would say.

She leaned forward onto his chest, eyes closed, feeling him lean over her, catch her behind the knees and pick her up into his arms. "You're so light," he whispered in a distracted way.

He carried her back into the bedroom and placed her on the bed. "I'm going to change the decor in this room," he muttered as he stood above her, removing his clothes.

Vona wanted to look away but her eyes seemed glued to that strong masculine body, sinewed like an athlete's. There was none of the softness of the office worker about Jake.

"I like the way you look at me, darling," Jake growled as he lowered himself beside her and began stripping the clothes from her body.

When she saw him look at her bra, she could feel a quiver of shame, which she quickly squelched. "It's been mended a few times, if that's what's going through your mind. But it's clean."

"Just like the rest of you." He tossed the object of perusal over his shoulder and buried his face between her breasts. "Your skin smells so sweet. I'd like to buy you enough lacy underwear to last you until you were an old lady...silk to cover you here, and here, and here..." His hands made circling forays up and down her body, lingering on her abdomen, the soft smallness of her waist. "Your bones are too prominent...." He kissed her hipbones, one side at a time, his lips lingering in a soft sucking motion.

"I've...I've never felt like this...." The words were pulled from her mouth. She had not wanted to tell Jake such a thing.

Even now, as the memory dredged her with ecstasy and pain, Siobhan writhed at how revealing she had been in her emotions to Jake that day. He plumbed her and found the core of love that she had buried there for him, and him alone.

Now she had changed. Her hair color was changed, her attitude had changed. Oh, she was still as tough as the old Vona had been—maybe even tougher. But there had been many outward changes. Like a chameleon, Siobhan had changed her colors and fitted herself into another environment. She would be invisible to Jake Deerfield. Maybe!

She sat up straight in the hot tub, sloshing some of the water onto the waterproof rim. For some reason, Jake's memory seemed to be smothering her tonight. It was as though the times they had made love, two years ago and last week, had merged and become one.

But her mind took her back through time and she watched a young Vona lose her shyness as she and Jake came together. Then she would skip to when she, as Siobhan, had made love with Jake just days earlier. She exhaled a shuddering sigh. There had been other men who had wanted to be her lovers and she had turned them away with ease, but with Jake she came alive, became a total sensualist.

Her reaction to him now, two years between their first and present lovemaking experiences, had been the same—a total commitment to giving him pleasure. She had struggled through her own fog of desire to give pleasure to the man who made her body rock with joy. "Why? Why did all the gods choose this man for me? Why can't another man find the love that's in me? Damn you, Jake Deerfield!" She closed her eyes on the groan, knowing she couldn't fight the memory.

"Jake...Jake...I love you," she had cried out in his arms when she was twenty-two.

"I want you to love me, darling, again...and again." But he didn't say that he loved her.

Once more Jake began to caress her, his mouth moving down her body as though he would mark it as his own. She knew that she could refuse him nothing. But that he could pleasure her so much, time after time, stunned her, weakened her, delighted her, strengthened her.

The shattering descent from the love plane had her body shaking as though she were ill. It stunned her when her feathering hand felt the same tremor in Jake's body.

"I think we have a most powerful chemistry, Vona Butler."

"I think so too." Her smile was out of control. It was as though all the joy in all her life had been unleashed.

ALL THROUGH the night, Jake ministered to her body, not letting her move, except to go to the bathroom.

The next day he insisted that she call the diner to tell them she wouldn't be in for a few days.

"I can't do that." Vona was up and dressing at five in the morning. "I need that job."

"What happens when you're sick?" A sleepy Jake quizzed her, a towel wrapped around his middle as he looked at her owlishly.

"I'm never sick. I take vitamins," Vona told him in all seriousness, frowning at him when he threw back his head and laughed.

"Well, tomorrow you are going to be sick. I'll take you in today, but tomorrow you're staying with me. I'll call in sick for you."

"Jake, I need this job."

"Stop worrying about the damned job." He growled at her, pulling on a pair of well-washed jeans after he dropped the towel, not bothering to don underwear or take note of her red face. "I'll eat breakfast with you when I drop you off."

"Oh, I don't get breakfast," Vona looked at him horrified. "I take a dinner, and that's all I'm allowed— one meal."

Jake took hold of her upper arms. "Are you telling me that you eat one meal a day and it's at night?"

Vona nodded. "I don't have time to eat," she bleated.

"You are going to eat, Vona, not a lot, but you are going to eat." Jake told her, grim-faced, as he pulled her into his kitchen.

What Jake considered "not a lot" flabbergasted Vona. He sliced her an orange and a banana, the banana over wheat cereal. Then there was toast and jam with a soft-boiled egg accompanied by a glass of orange juice, vitamins, and instant coffee.

"Eat," Jake threatened, sitting next to her and buttering her toast, then dolloping peach jam over it.

"I'll burst!" Vona spooned the last of the cereal into her mouth.

"You have a long way to go before you come apart. And you have a damned good appetite that should be appeased."

"You sound like my instructor in Nutrition Class."

Jake smiled at her, then leaned over and licked peach jam from her lips. "Mustn't be messy."

"Right," Vona breathed, seeing stars, pinwheels and comets behind her eyes.

Jake came with her when she went upstairs to brush her teeth.

"I don't have my toothbrush with me," Vona tried to explain.

Jake laughed. "I didn't think that you did." He opened a drawer in the bathroom vanity and pulled out a brand-new toothbrush still in its plastic wrapper.

"I've never been in a house where they keep boxes of toothbrushes before," Vona muttered, staring at her lathered mouth. "This is not your world, Vona Butler...." She spoke in low tones, knowing that Jake was in the bedroom getting a shirt and that he might be able to hear her talking to herself. "I wonder what mother and the kids would think of me in a house like this," Vona spoke to her mirror image. "She'd tell me to get my backside out of here at top speed." Vona laughed, some of the water she was splashing onto her face dripping down her chin. "Mother would have given James Kendall Deerfield the tongue-lashing of his life by now," Vona chuckled.

"I like to hear you laugh." Jake pushed open the bathroom door and looked at her.

"You won't like what I was thinking," Vona stated, her heart doing a full loop when he smiled at her.

"I won't?" When he stretched his arms, his chest pushed against the fabric of the sport shirt he was wearing.

"No. I was thinking that my mother would have your hide—and mine—because I'm here."

"Tough lady, your mother?" Jake drawled.

"Tough enough to put you in line if she needed to," Vona stated, feeling her chin thrust forward.

"Whoa, baby, let's not battle—unless we're in bed." Jake reached out an arm to snag her close to his body, his mouth feathering down her face.

"Have to get to work." Vona pushed the words out.

"I know," he whispered. "Just cuddling you a bit for warmth."

"I'm warm," she gulped.

"Then warm me, baby."

"Jake . . ." Vona pleaded, feeling her calf muscles liquify.

"All right, you win. But tomorrow, we stay in bed." Jake hugged her and didn't see her face.

Vona clutched him to her, knowing that her face was twisted with all the things she wasn't telling him. She didn't tell him that she would be gone that day, that she was only working half a shift, then catching a bus to Manhattan. She didn't tell him that Hughy would be meeting that bus and would be personally seeing to the overhaul of Vona Butler. It was better that she and Jake part this way—quick and sure. She didn't belong in his world. She knew it, and she was sure that he did.

As he drove her to work, she wondered what it would

be like to go to school in New York City to finish her degree, instead of going to the State University at New Paltz. She had already arranged for the transfer of her credits. Hughy had found her a one-room apartment. He had talked to a friend of his about her acting lessons, modeling, makeup. . . .

"You're quiet, angel." Jake squeezed her knee as he pulled up in front of the diner. "See you later."

"Yes. See you later." She reached for him with both hands, bringing his face to hers, opening her mouth on his, letting her soul touch his.

Jake held her when she would have stepped out of the car. "What's wrong, Vona?"

"Nothing." She freed herself and left the car, running into the diner.

In the afternoon, she had taken the bus and left New Paltz, never to return, her eyes burning with unshed tears because she was leaving Jake and she loved him.

A groaning Siobhan sat straight up in the tub again. "No, no, I don't love him. He's not part of my life any more. I've exorcised him. . . ." She pushed one fist into the palm of her other hand, splashing water.

"What the hell are you mumbling about? And more to the point, what the bloody hell are you doing in my hot tub? I've been looking for you."

Siobhan was sure she had stepped through the Looking Glass into a first-class nightmare as she looked up and up into Jake Deerfield's face, a Jake Deerfield of flesh and bone, and not of her imagining.

SIOBHAN SPUTTERED, her words like marbles loose in her mind, not coming together in any clear way.

Jake began disrobing, not taking his eyes off her. "I have been searching this damned continent for you, and here you are with Hughy at Deerfield Hall."

"Surprise, surprise," she choked, starting to rise. "Just give me a minute and you can have the tub to yourself." She reached for her wrap, but it was snatched from her hand.

"No way, angel. Now that I have you here, I'm keeping you here. A good long soak in that tub is just what I need after that drive from New York."

"No..." Siobhan slid to the far side of the tub and tried to rise, grabbing for a bath sheet. She gaped at the speed with which he removed his clothes.

Jake's hand shot out and manacled her wrist. "Relax, angel, I'm not going to assault you. Take that scared look off your face. I realize I went too fast for you the first time around." He eased her back into the water, then followed her down into the frothy depths of the tub, smiling at her. "I'm not going to hurt you, even though I was damned angry for days when I couldn't find you at first. Then I figured out that I was coming on a little strong with you." His grin almost sent her into cardiac arrest. She didn't know this Jake Deerfield.

"Ah—I was planning to go back to New York and let

Hughy have more privacy." She coughed to try to clear the huskiness from her voice.

"Ah yes," Jake leaned his head back and closed his eyes. "My old school chum, Hugh Varner Prentice." He sighed. "I owe him one."

"No, you don't," she protested. "I asked Hughy to hide me out up here, so I could rest and think about . . . a part . . . I'm considering. . . ." Siobhan felt impaled when those sapphire eyes flew open and stared at her.

"I called here twice and said I was looking for you."

"I told him not to put any calls through to me. It wasn't Hughy's fault and I won't have you starting something with him. It was wrong of me to come here . . . and I'll be getting out. . . ."

"No way. You're staying—but so am I."

"Hughy won't be able to concentrate."

"Then *he* can get out." Jake frowned at her, a strange look in his eyes.

"What is it?" she breathed, sure that he finally recognized her.

"I don't know. I had the feeling I've played this scene before with you." He stared at her. "It must be the eyes. You have eyes just like . . . an old friend of mine."

"A woman," she stated, ready to tell him that she was Vona Butler.

"No—a child. A child of the streets."

Her lips locked on the hurt that welled up. So that's what he thought of her! To him she had just been a tramp. She didn't give a damn what he thought, she would tell him she was Vona Butler, then get away from him.

She rose up out of the water so fast that Jake didn't have time to stop her.

Then his gaze was frozen on her. "Your body is so beautiful, it reminds me—"

"I find your waltz down Memory Lane a bit tedious and boring, Mr. Deerfield. Please do not include me in any more of your maudlin stories. . . ." She grabbed the bath sheet, whirled it around her body like a cape and stomped from the room, Jake not moving from where he was, his eyes still glued to her.

Back in her room, she tried to force down the dry sobs that rose in her throat, tearing and ripping her insides as they fought free of her body. Finally, she went to the bathroom and lost her dinner.

The knock at her bedroom door brought her from the bathroom, still wrapped in the bath sheet she had taken from Jake's apartments, wiping her mouth on a tissue.

"Siobhan. . . Siobhan, let me in. Are you all right?"

"No, I'm not all right. I would like to be left alone. Go away."

"Are you crying?"

"Go away. . . go away. . . ." She stared at the door dry-eyed, hating Jake Deerfield.

For what seemed like hours, she sat on the side of her bed and stared at the wall, trying to marshal her life and thoughts.

She was still sitting like that when she heard Hughy's Mercedes come up the drive. Galvanized into action, she seized her silk dressing gown and pulled it over her nude body, pushing her feet into fluffy mules.

She yanked a comb so hard through her hair that tears sprang to her eyes, then she left the room at a clip-clopping gallop, stumbling in the awkward slippers.

As she reached the top of the stairs, Maura came in the door. She was looking over her shoulder, laughing and speaking to someone behind her.

"Maura...Maura...listen..." Siobhan started down the stairs as Hughy and Lance followed Maura into the house. The three of them looked up at her, smiles still on their faces. "Listen...."

"What is it?" Hughy walked toward the stairs.

"The worst..." Siobhan trembled as Maura hurried to her side.

"She means the jig is up, Hughy," Jake drawled, strolling from the library, saluting his friend with the glass in his hand. Only the slightest furrowing of his brow acknowledged the presence of the other two, his interest seeming to zero in on Siobhan, then Hughy.

"Jake! What the hell?" Hughy began, color running up his neck.

"Is this Jake?" Lance inquired, not intimidated by the large black-haired man with the twisted smile on his face.

"I am. I have no intention of asking you what you have heard about me, Mr...."

"Butler. Lance Butler." Lance moved forward, hand outstretched, only slightly discomfited when Jake only stared at him, his hand staying at his side for a moment.

"Oh, yes. How are you?" Jake shook the proffered hand, still staring hard at Lance. "I used to know someone by the name of Butler...."

"And I'm Maura Butler..." Maura held out her hand, open curiosity on her face.

"And I'm Siobhan Ryan Butler, sometimes called Vona," Siobhan said in a toneless voice.

Can silence be thunderous? Vona wondered, strangely detached, as Jake whirled to face her like a pugilist at the ready, teeth bared, fist cocked, eyes narrowed.

"No!" Jake bellowed.

The other three turned to statues as the antagonists came out of their corners, both eager for mayhem.

"You are a liar, my little dove." Jake's voice was sibilant and dangerous. "Why didn't you tell me right away who you were?"

"How is it that you didn't recognize me? Or is it that the parade of whores through this house has been so great...that you couldn't possibly remember one from the other?" Siobhan spat the words at him as she slowly came down the steps.

"You damn well aren't going to get away with calling my sister names." Lance started forward, his face fluctuating from white to red.

Hughy took hold of his upper arms, restraining him.

"Too right about that," Maura growled, rushing forward to kick Jake in the shinbone. "You insult one Butler, boyo, you insult us all."

"Too right." Lance flailed his arms, trying to get around Hughy.

"Who the hell are they?" Jake lifted his leg and rubbed his shin.

"They are my brother and sister and they're leaving with me this very minute." Siobhan's raised voice had a quaver in it.

"No." Jake roared again, stopping all movement and speech. "No one is leaving, and certainly not you, my sweet Vona. You have a great deal to explain."

"I owe you no explanation, you—you creep," Siobhan shot at him, now on the bottom stair.

"What the hell did I ever do to you?"

"I'm too much of a lady to say."

"What?" Lance and Maura shouted before starting for Jake again.

"Stop, damn you. All of you, stop!" Hughy yelled,

anger in every line of his body. "This has turned into a damned donnybrook and nobody is listening to anybody."

In the silence, rasping breath was the only sound.

"All right," Jake inhaled. "No one is leaving tonight. It's too late and tempers are frayed. We'll drink the coffee Mrs. White has set out in the library, then we'll go to bed and talk in the morning."

"Coffee keeps me awake." Siobhan felt a strong desire to punch Jake Deerfield in the nose.

"It's decaffeinated," Hughy placated, taking Maura's arm and urging Lance ahead of him toward the door.

"If you make one move...." Lance grated as he passed Jake.

"Have your sister pour the coffee," Jake instructed, not taking his eyes from Siobhan.

"I will not stay after tomorrow," she glared at him, just a hair taller than he as she stood on the last step.

"We have to talk," Jake murmured. "Dammit, it was a shock. I knew there was something about you, but...."

"I will agree to nothing except leaving here. You have no hold over me," Siobhan flung at him.

"I like the name Siobhan better than Vona," Jake whispered.

"My father always called me Siobhan," she responded, feeling prickly all over her body.

"I didn't know how to pronounce it until I asked Hughy."

"It's Gaelic. Daddy used to say that it sounds like the word shove with 'on' at the end, putting the accent at the end. Shove-on."

Jake nodded. "It's beautiful. Is that the true color of your hair, not the red you told me it was?"

She nodded, shifting her weight from one foot to the other. "Hughy and the rest will be waiting for us." She walked past him, down one step, feeling her body brush his when he wouldn't step aside.

"The moment we met, I knew there was something, but I didn't know what it was."

She paused, but didn't turn around, then continued into the library, the others looking up at once when she entered.

"What made you come down here, Jake?" Hughy asked, the only one eating the little cakes set out on the table.

"I called you to see..." Jake stopped. "When Mrs. White said you were in and that you were riding with the young man, I decided to drive up and see who was visiting you. I thought we could have a talk about some personal matters." He looked at Siobhan, then back at Hughy. "I'll talk to you later."

Siobhan began to feel uncomfortable under his scrutiny. "My brother and sister and I will be leaving tomorrow."

"Ah...sis...I just signed up..." Lance began, but was silenced by her look.

"There's no need for anyone to leave. I said that before." Jake took the coffee proffered him by Maura and quickly drank it down scalding hot with no cream or sugar. "This house is very large and geared to handle five times the people here now. Mrs. White must be delighted with the crew, eh, Hughy?"

Hughy stared at his friend, his eyes narrowed. "She seems pleased."

"Good. Then I think we can all get to bed." Jake stood there, his hands shoved into his jacket pockets, his eyes on Siobhan again.

She wheeled at once, going out to the hall and up the stairs, calling to Maura to come with her, but not turning to see if she was there.

"You can't hide forever, Siobhan." Jake's soft words coiled out to her like a satin lariat, as he stood at the foot of the stairs.

"Good night," she said through her teeth, hearing her sister behind her.

Maura followed her into the room and closed the door. "What the hell went on between you two?"

"An experience I'd prefer to forget." Siobhan sat down at the vanity and began to brush her hair, trying to get out the snarls caused by letting it dry without combing or brushing.

"I don't think I'd like messing with him. He's so sinister!" Maura gave a breathless laugh.

Her sister's hand stopped in mid-stroke, her eyes flying to Maura's face in the mirror. "That's an apt description of Mr. Deerfield."

"He said we were to call him Jake," Maura grinned, then yawned. "I'm going to have a quick wash, then it's bed for me."

To Siobhan's surprise, she fell asleep, but only to dream. The girl in her dream wasn't recognizable until she came close, for she kept looking over her shoulder. It was herself, and Jake was chasing her, running and laughing and closing fast.

When she woke in the gray pre-dawn, her body was moist with perspiration. One hand shook as she wiped it across her face. "Damn you, Jake Deerfield, you won't get me this time."

She fell into a fitful sleep, to dream of being jounced around on the back of a pickup truck, her teeth rattling as the vehicle swung back and forth.

"Hey, sleepyhead, we're going riding. . ." Maura bent over her.

"Oh, you were rocking me," Siobhan mumbled. "I was dreaming that I was in the back of a truck getting bounced around." She yawned when her sister laughed but her own laugh, mixed with the yawn, was abruptly cut off as she remembered. Jake was here! She had been about to tell Maura that she was going to skip the morning ride, but the thought of seeing Jake at breakfast was enough to change her mind. "Just let me catch a quick shower and I'll go with you."

"Have you changed your mind about riding, then?"

"No, I haven't," Siobhan called from the bathroom. "But I decided that since the family was so involved, I should learn, too."

"Sweet," Maura stuck her head into the shower cubicle. "But I don't buy it." She ducked when Siobhan tossed a wet face cloth her way. "I'll see you down at the stables."

Siobhan gritted her teeth as she pulled on the jeans that she used for riding, her skin protesting. "Why do I do this, knowing that I'll be in agony afterward? Why do people think that riding a horse is so great? I think it's awful." She tucked her still-damp hair into a kerchief knotted at the back of her head, buttoned the cuff of her man-style plaid shirt, put on a suede vest and slipped into her loafers. Then she padded down the stairs to the front door, where she was greeted by the sun, shining with an eye-blinking glare. But the breeze was cold, and she shivered, then decided to go back for her jacket.

"Here you are, darling. I thought you might need it." Before she could turn around at the sound of his voice, Jake had put a hip-length suede jacket around her. "Before you start asking questions, it belongs to my sister."

"You have a sister?" Siobhan gulped, looking away from those navy-blue eyes.

"I have a sister, yes, plus the two-parent requirement for all of the above." Jake leaned over her and kissed her ear.

"Don't talk down to me, you—"

"Easy, precious, easy." The hard amusement in Jake's eyes didn't quiver when she clenched her fists. "Come on, lady, the horses are waiting."

"How do you know?" Siobhan dug in her heels.

"This is my home. As a rule I know what's going on here. Admittedly, Hughy put one over on me, but . . . ."

"I don't ride well. I think I'll eat." Siobhan turned away to enter the house, but felt herself lifted back against a hard-muscled body. "I really am hungry," she insisted.

"Good. I arranged for Amos to have some food for you, before you ride. A little fruit, some juice. . . ." Jake kept his arm around her as he turned her and led her down the steps to a path that would take them around to the stables. "Amos says that you're doing better every day and that you and Nancy are good friends."

"He exaggerates," Siobhan gulped. "She puts up with me, but I'm not any better at riding than I was the first day. The others just go off and let Nancy and me plod up and down the woods path."

"Today you'll have me with you," Jake promised. Waving the riding crop in his hand at Hughy, Maura and Lance, he told them, "Go ahead. I'll take her with me."

"No need," Siobhan whispered. "You go with them. Really, I would prefer it. Then Nancy and I could have a nice chat."

"You chat with the horses? Nice. Today you can chat

with me," Jake chuckled. "Wave to them." He gestured to where the three others had begun to canter from the stable yard.

Siobhan lifted her hand and flapped it toward the moving horses, but her attention was on the coal-black horse, at least thirty feet high she estimated, that Amos and a young man were holding. "Is this a suicide mission?" The words were pushed through tight lips.

"Not to worry, love. It's just Faust's way of saying he missed me."

"Cute."

Jake half lifted, half dragged her forward, then gave her a leg up onto the placid Nancy, who turned her head once to see who was getting on her back. "There you are, darling. How does that feel?"

"High." She wasn't looking at Jake. She was watching Faust as he plunged and whinnied. When Jake took the reins from Amos and swung into the saddle, her heart dropped a thousand feet and bounced up again. "Be careful." She barely mouthed the words.

"Ready, love?"

Siobhan nodded and leaned over Nancy's neck. "Pay no attention to that black show-off. He isn't nearly as sweet as you," she whispered to the horse, whose ears flicked back and forth. Then the mare moved out in her mincing walk, her rider swaying in the saddle.

"I'll be right back, darling. I'm going to gallop Faust for a minute so that he won't be so jumpy."

"Don't hurry back," Siobhan muttered, trying to shift her leg so that the most chafed section of skin was lifted free of the horse.

Nancy took it as a signal to go faster. In minutes, Siobhan was bouncing up and down and sideways as she tried to pull back on the reins. It seemed that Nancy was feeling a bit of spring fever, Siobhan thought, as her hands slipped on the reins and the horse kept moving at a slow canter. "Heavens, Nancy, stop, will you. Every tooth in my head is loose and I have a ringing in my ears. . . ." Her words caromed back to her as though she had just spoken out loud on a roller coaster. Her voice was disjointed, and out of rhythm.

"Whoa. Where are you going, pretty lady?" Jake leaned down and with minimum pressure on the reins brought Nancy to a stop. He was laughing until he saw Siobhan wince. "Are your legs chafed, love?"

She nodded.

"I'll fix that." With surprising agility, he swung his leg over the horse's head and slid off his back. Then he returned to Siobhan, lifted her from the saddle to the ground, turned Nancy around and slapped her rump. "She'll go back to the barn," he informed an open-mouthed Siobhan.

"And what do I do, flag down a cab?" she quizzed, watching the retreating backside of the easygoing Nancy.

Jake grinned and led her to Faust's side. "Don't hang back. He's a very nice fellow when you get to know him."

"Comforting," she mumbled, watching Jake swing up into the saddle, then reach down a hand to her. "I hope that's your way of saying so long," she quipped.

"Put your foot on my boot. No, not that foot, the other one. Give me your hand."

She felt herself lifted into the air, then settled in front of Jake on the saddle, both her legs on one side of the horse, instead of straddled. "Will the horse mind?" she gulped, more disturbed by the body pressed to hers than by the horse beneath her.

"I don't think so. He's strong and could carry more weight than the two of us," Jake told her. "Comfortable?"

"Relatively." She refused to tell him that it felt wonderful to be moving forward in such a fashion.

"You're mine, you know," Jake stated in a conversational manner.

"What? Don't be silly." She stiffened when Faust tossed his head, his forward motion strong and sure.

"Relax, darling. Lean back, you'll be more comfortable. That's the way." They rode together in silence.

It surprised her how comfortable she felt, situated as she was in front of Jake. After a few more moments she settled against him.

"If it were warmer I would dismount from this horse and make love to you under those trees. Or haven't you noticed the effect you've had on me, my love?" He grasped her tightly so she could feel his excitement.

"I'd better walk," Siobhan squirmed.

"No way." Jake chuckled into her neck. "Do you know how long I wondered what had happened to you, and how I was going to find you?"

"Until you found the next waitress?" Siobhan snapped, trying to rally her defenses.

The tightening of his hand at her waist made her exclaim; the horse, reacting to the sound, reared and whinnied, making Siobhan cry out again.

For long moments, Jake fought with the disgruntled black. Then Faust settled into the easy-motion trot. "See, darling. Everything is taken care of—by me—and that's the way it will be from now on. And don't make cutesy remarks about the women in my life. If you want to know about them, ask. I will probably tell you that it's none of your business, but ask anyway."

"You damned rutting aristocrat." She sounded out each syllable, not caring if he dumped her on the ground.

"Have I asked you about the men in your life since we parted?" Jake breathed into her neck.

"I've lost count. Give me a day and I'll be able to come up with most of the names—hey, let go!" Siobhan was held so tightly that she couldn't wiggle.

"Stop pushing your luck . . ." snapped Jake.

"Don't you threaten me . . . you . . . you leftover from the Kama Sutra. You have no hold over me," she panted, a mixture of fear and anger filling her.

"Stop it, Siobhan."

"Did you know I heard your discussing me in the diner with Hughy?" Dark memories seeped to the top of her mind like oil surfacing from the ground. "Did you know I heard you tell Hughy that I was a sow's ear?"

"Siobhan, stop it. That's ancient history. I was a fool."

Suddenly, the horse sidled and whinnied, throwing his head.

"Let's calm down. Then Faust will be calm," Jake assured her, whistling to the horse. "Siobhan, I admit that I acted like a fool—"

"We were both of us fools," she interrupted.

Jake cuddled her back against his body as they returned down the sloping path that would take them to the stable. "We'll talk again, love. There's plenty to say."

"I'm going back to New York, Jake, and . . ."

"And your role as Raine," Jake finished.

"No, I'm not keeping that job. I've decided to broaden my horizons. Zenith has a script that I've been reading. I like it. . . ."

" 'Day by Day' is top-rated. You can't afford to just chuck it." Jakes' voice was hard.

"There are other jobs in the industry."

"None better than that, and you know it."

Much to Siobhan's relief, Lance galloped up the hill to meet them. "You weren't tumbled, were you?" There was rigid concern on his face.

"No. My legs were chafing me. Jake thought I should ride home this way to prevent further rubbing," she assured her brother.

"Is that what I thought?" Jake drawled in her ear.

"That's some horse, Jake. How many hands?"

"Sixteen."

"Lance stared hungrily at the sleekly moving animal.

"Would you like to ride him one day?" Jake asked as he reined in the horse in front of the stable, then slid from its back, putting up his hands to lift Siobhan down in front of him. He kept hold of her as he nodded at one of the grooms to curry the horse.

"You're not just pulling my leg, are you?" Lance was in shock.

"No. When Amos says you're ready to ride him, you may. I mean that." Jake hadn't released Siobhan. "Now let's get some breakfast. Siobhan is starving as usual." He chuckled when she glared at him.

"Back home in Australia, my mum was always telling us to eat everything on our plates the way Vona did." Maura giggled, as she and Hughy walked over to them.

"All of the Butlers have appetites, if I remember right," Siobhan shot back.

"Yes. Andrew used to say that the greatest incentive to success was the thought of how many mouths he had to feed," Lance laughed.

"You sound as though you're fond of your father," Jake said, walking with his arm around Siobhan.

"He's a great gun—just like a real father to all of us," Lance nodded.

"Yes, he is," Maura agreed. "In fact, when something went wrong, more than likely we would go to Andrew. Mum is great, but she's out of her depth if you discuss anything more intimate than her recipe for pie crust."

Siobhan nodded, laughing with the others. But she remembered the pain of wanting to discuss "girl things" with her mother, and being fobbed off by her embarrassed parent. She had never doubted her mother's love for her, but she'd often wished that her mother had been able to communicate better.

When she shook herself from the reverie, a shivering awareness told her that Jake was watching her. She tried to free herself from him and follow the others into breakfast, but he was with her, step by step.

"You were lonely, even in your large family, weren't you, Siobhan?"

"Yes. Sometimes I felt caught in a marshmallow jail. I could never tell my mother how I felt. Nor could I talk to . . . ." Her tongue clove to the roof of her mouth as she realized that some of her deepest thoughts had come out.

"I was often lonely too, yet I knew my parents loved me. It was as though we were trains traveling on parallel tracks—close, but not touching."

"Yes," Siobhan bit her lip on the sob.

"You see, we are alike, my darling Siobhan," Jake breathed as he ushered her into the dining room, where Maura and Lance were having a raucous conversation about who had really won the race at the district fair.

"They called it a dead heat, after all," Maura pointed out.

"Sandy Davis won it, Maur—everyone who was there says that. Dylan Lane was on a better horse, but he's not the horseman Sandy is."

"A fair dinkum lad is our Sandy," mimicked Maura, making Lance's jaw jut forward.

"You look just like Siobhan when you do that," Jake told Lance, turning the eyes of the people at the table toward him as he pushed Siobhan's chair into the table, then kissed her on the top of the head.

She stiffened at the assessing looks of her brother and sister. "Tell me more about this Sandy Davis, the horseman."

"Ahhh, c'mon Vona, you don't want to hear about Sandy," Lance looked disgusted. "You're just trying to put us off watching you and Jake."

"There's nothing to watch..." she began, then reddened when Jake chuckled.

"They can see right through you, darling."

Siobhan whirled on him as he filled a plate for her at the sideboard and brought it to the table. "I'll help myself, thank you. Don't you dare imply that there is something between us." She didn't even look away when Hughy hissed her name.

Mrs. White pushed her head around the door leading to the kitchen. "Did you call me, sir?"

"No, Mrs. White. Everything is fine." Jake answered blandly.

When Mrs. White had disappeared again, Siobhan jumped to her feet, took the plate that Jake had filled, and set it in front of his place. Then she turned toward the food on the sideboard and began to fill another plate.

"What's going on?" Maura's question bounced off the wall.

"I think we are about to have a food war," Hughy answered in flat tones.

"There is nothing going on..." Siobhan turned to glower at Hughy for a moment, then went back to spooning the orange and grapefruit sections into a dish. "I am just telling anyone who cares to listen that there could never be anything going on between me and a man who bet another man that I would be impossible to improve or teach anything...."

"Siobhan," Jake surged to his feet, "You know damn well I did that out of caprice. I was hung over that day. You know damn well none of that meant anything to me later."

"I know you said all the money in the world couldn't turn *that* sow's ear into a silk purse..." Siobhan turned around and leaned back against the sideboard, trying to control her breathing. "I remember that you pointed right at me."

"Siobhan, that was years ago. I looked for you—"

"I'm sure you did. You did tell me I was good for one thing—"

"Siobhan..." Jake roared.

"Vona..." Lance shouted at the same time, jumping to his feet and knocking his chair backward.

"That's done it," Hughy remarked, dabbing at his mouth with his napkin, then getting up to grab Lance by the upper arms.

"Let me go, Hughy. I'm not going to kill him." Lance ground out, "...but I am going to land him a facer for what he said about Vona."

"No," Hughy took a stronger grip. "Not only wouldn't you land a punch," he spoke through a clenched jaw, "but Jake would probably take you apart. Pay attention to me. I know Jake. I haven't seen him this angry in years."

Hughy and Lance both turned to look at the man in question.

Jake hadn't taken his eyes from Siobhan, but now a dark red stained his face, a muscle jumping in his cheek, his eyes furious slits. "You know damn well I never felt that way about you after—"

"Shut up!" she shouted, her trembling hand lifting the dish of fruit as though she would throw it.

"Go ahead," Jake whispered, his stance threatening.

"Don't think I won't," she snapped back.

"Vona..." Maura stood. "Vona...you never lose your temper...." Her mouth was agape as she watched her older sister. "Nothing ever made you give way."

Siobhan's eyes slid toward her sister, then her hand wavered and came down in front of her, the slight tremor making the fruit slide around the dish. "On second thought, I don't feel like eating." She set down her dishes.

Jake scowled at her. "You're eating. You're too thin." He was around the table and at her side. "Please. Eat. Just a little fruit and some toast."

Siobhan looked from her sister to her brother to Hughy and felt ashamed of her actions. "I'll have some juice."

For long moments the only sounds in the morning room were of cutlery hitting plates and an occasional cough or swallow.

"Ah, Jake, the book is going so well that I think that I'll go back to the city with the Butlers." Hughy dabbed at the corner of his mouth with his napkin.

"Fine. Your car will be full. I'll take Lance with me."

Jake turned around to look fully at the boy. "You'd like to drive a Ferrari, wouldn't you?"

"A real Ferrari?" Lance groaned, his eyes popping.

"I should say..." Hughy interjected. "That damn thing goes from zero to a hundred in milliseconds."

"Don't you dare drive like that," Siobhan looked at her younger brother.

"I'm sure Lance has too much sense to ever drive like that." Jake pronounced, earning a gratified glance from the boy and an angry, suspicious one from Siobhan. He looked back at her, smiling blandly.

"Well, that's settled then." Hughy rose, coming around the table to help Maura from her chair. "We'll leave in the early afternoon?"

The ride back to New York that afternoon promised to be an ordeal until Siobhan realized that Hughy and Maura were aware only of each other. Satisfied, she leaned against the car door and tried to nap.

Manhattan in the afternoon was tooting horns and squealing brakes, horror to most of the people snarled there. Maura thought it was heaven.

"I had no idea it was like this..." she exclaimed, craning her neck left and right to see everything. "How lucky you are to live here all the time."

Siobhan had to smile, remembering her first starry-eyed view of the Big Apple when Hughy had brought her to town. "It is wonderful—"

"Some of the time," Hughy interrupted, throwing fond glances at Maura sitting so close to him. "Many times it's just insanity."

"I'll love it," Maura told him firmly, squeezing his arm.

When Hughy swung the car around the corner and down into the darkness of the underground garage, Maura laughed with delight.

For Siobhan, it was a relief that the ride was over and she could get back to her own apartment.

"Siobhan . . ." Hughy said as he lifted the suitcases out of the trunk. "I was thinking that it might be more comfortable all around if I took Lance to stay with me. That way, you and Maura wouldn't be so crowded." Hughy lined the cases up next to the elevator just as the Ferrari came down into the garage.

"Actually," Maura pinched Hughy's cheeks, "I tried to get him to take me into his apartment, Vona, but he turned me down . . . boo hoo. . . ."

"Not true . . ." Hughy looked at her, about to reply. But before he could say anything Lance was hopping out of the Ferrari and running toward them.

"Vona . . . Maura . . . what a car! Jake says I can take you out in it some time. I drove it that well, he said. Jake says that I can stay with him and that I can have a car to drive to school here, too. He says there's so much room in his apartment I'll get lost." Lance finished on a whoosh of air, making Maura laugh.

Siobhan stared at the expressionless Jake, who was leaning on the passenger side of the car, his arms folded on his chest. "I think that Lance should stay with Hughy. . . ." she countered.

"He wants to go college. He'll need a car," Jake shrugged.

"He can take a bus, or the subway." She gritted her teeth.

"I offered my extra room for Lance." Hughy looked at his friend narrow-eyed. "Then he would be near his sisters."

"He won't be that far, living with me," Jake said in a flat voice. "I thought we would go down to Columbia this afternoon and see what he could audit before taking the summer courses. If he stays out on the Island at my folks' summer home, it's an easy commute in by—"

"What makes you think that I would let my brother stay with you—let alone at your parents' home." Siobhan leaned toward Jake, her hands clenched at her side.

"Ah, Vona, don't spoil it. Jake and I talked all the way into town and he said that he might have a part-time job for me in his organization. . . ." Lance pleaded.

" 'Murder Incorporated'?" she inquired.

Jake inclined his head, his eyes glittering over her. "Darling, how you talk."

Siobhan shuddered as she felt an invisible silken net closing over her, tightening, smothering her.

5

Siobhan went back to work as Raine on "Day by Day" but she asked Hughy to get her phased out of the show. "I've decided that I want to do that show for Zenith."

Hughy sat with his feet up on his desk, facing her. "I have a feeling that you left it too late—"

The door crashed open and Maura burst in, her smile beaming from Siobhan to Hughy. "I got the job. You are looking at the new receptionist for this building, folks."

Hughy's feet crashed to the floor and he stood up and came around the desk. "Congratulations, brat," he said as he kissed her full on the mouth.

When Maura's arms went around Hughy's neck and the kiss continued, Siobhan coughed...and coughed again. Then she shuffled her feet and finally stood up. "Hey, you two. I think what you're doing borders on the illegal."

Maura turned her head, grinning. "That's all right. I asked him to marry me last night."

"And I accepted." Hughy's grin looked even more foolish with the smear of lip gloss on it.

Maura frowned up at him, wiping his mouth with one finger. "I don't understand. The lady at the cosmetic counter promised me that it was smearproof."

Siobhan laughing, grabbed at Hughy's hand and squeezed it hard. "I don't think she realized that you would be trying to laminate yourself to a man while wearing it."

"What will your mother say, Siobhan?" Hughy looked worried.

"I told him that Mother would love him," Maura crooned to her intended.

"I agree with Maura," Siobhan kissed Hughy full on the mouth just as the door opened and Jake walked into the room.

"What the hell is going on?" The velvet bite to the words sent a shiver down Siobhan's spine.

"It's about Hughy's forthcoming marriage." Maura's smile had an impish glint.

"Who are you marrying?" Jake's voice could have stopped the clock in the room.

"Me. Who else?" Maura laughed.

Jake looked at her. His hard smile briefly touched everyone, then came back to Maura again. "Very timely." He leaned back against the closed door. "I'm getting engaged myself soon."

Siobhan's heart dropped into her shoes, then popped back into place again, its pace slowing to the speed of a slug. Every nerve end was being lacerated as she fought to keep the pain from showing on her face. 'Congratulations."

"Thank you. My parents are giving a small party to announce it at their home on the Island. You are all invited."

"I'll be busy. . . ."

"It's Saturday evening. . ." Jake continued blandly.

"Oh." Siobhan cleared her throat, feeling a painful relief. "I have plans with Lance that evening."

"Yes, I know." Jake continued. "He told me he'd bring you along with him when he came to the party. I'll already be at the house by the time you arrive." Jake looked at Hughy. "I understand from my mother that your parents will be coming and the Atwells and Cummings as well. . . ."

Hughy put his arm around Maura. "My love, you're going to be paraded before the family sooner than I expected." He kissed her on the head. "They'll love you."

Siobhan felt a giant hand twist and squeeze her inside. "I'm sorry, I won't . . . ."

"Maura will want you there as moral support, I should think," Jake said in mild tones.

"Oh yes, sis, don't fail me. I hadn't planned on meeting Hughy's family so soon." Maura looked wide-eyed and white for a moment.

"You'll want to go shopping, no doubt," Jake prodded.

"Mind your own . . ." Siobhan took a deep breath.

"Yes, sweetheart, you'll want the works." Hughy reached for his wallet, only to have Maura stop his hand. "Not that I care if you come in a brown paper bag." Hughy looked at her lovingly.

Siobhan stared at Jake, then moved closer to him. "I really don't want to come."

"Don't throw a wrench in Maura's good time." Jake looked down his patrician nose at her. "You want her to have a good time, don't you?"

"Of course, I do, but . . . ."

"Well, then, help her shop and buy something for yourself. Shall I give you some money?"

"I have plenty of money of my own." Siobhan breathed sulfurous fumes.

"Good." Jake smiled at her, steel chips in the look. "Then I'll see all of you Saturday." He went out slamming the door, leaving Siobhan biting her lip, her fingers knotting painfully.

Neither Maura nor Hughy noticed her. They were too busy looking at and holding each other.

"Siobhan...." Hughy patted his beloved on the shoulder. "I want you to take her to Chouchou's and let her get anything she wants." He looked down at Maura in a tender fashion. "It delights me to think that I am going to have her for a lifetime, to buy crazy things for, to indulge...."

"Mother would not want us indulged," Maura leaned on him, sighing. "In fact you may have to give away some of your money if you have too much. Mother considers it very selfish to have a great deal of money and not share it with the poor."

Siobhan nodded her head when Hughy looked up at her aghast. "True."

"Wow." Hughy looked thoughtful. "Well, if I must, I must. So, my love, get out there and spend some of my money, so that I'll have less when I meet your family."

Siobhan had been prepared to argue that Chouchou's was too expensive, when she remembered a far-out ensemble she had seen there a few weeks ago. She decided then and there she would try to get the outfit.

Maura was walking on air when they left Hughy's office. "Isn't he wonderful? I never in one million years thought I would find someone like my Hughy," she cooed as they stepped from the elevator to the lobby of the building. She pointed to a round raised dais with a switchboard in the center. "That's where I'll be working come Monday."

Her sister smiled and hurried her out to the street. 'It's only five blocks down, but I do have to get back and go over my lines this afternoon."

Maura was entranced with Fifth Avenue and she dawdled and gaped at everything. She insisted on stopping to get a drink of orange juice, smacking her lips. "What a super idea! A juice cart on the street."

"You are a worse tourist than I was when I came." Siobhan laughed, pulling at her arm. "And I was bad."

"New York is awesome, though," Maura laughed back, her head swiveling back and forth, and up and down.

When Siobhan stopped and pushed open a door beneath a small marquee, the door curtained in cream sheers, Maura blinked, then her mouth dropped at the elegant interior all done in creams and pale greens.

"Blimey, you could drown in the carpet," Maura whispered as a pencil-slim woman in black with pince-nez on a black ribbon approached them.

"Hello, I'm Siobhan Ryan from WEW and I would like to speak to Chouchou." She didn't smile at the woman, giving back her haughty stare.

The woman inclined her head a fraction. "I'll see if she's free."

The woman disappeared and Maura rolled her eyes at her sister.

"I think she thinks we're low-class," Maura said out of the side of her mouth.

"Don't feel bad. She feels that the Queen of England is her inferior. So we're in good company." Siobhan smiled at her sister who giggled.

Curtains at the far end of the room were flung back and a doll-like figure with short-cropped, silky black hair swept into the room, tottering on four-inch heels. "Siobhan, *ma chère*, you have come back to have your clothes made by an expert, *hein. Dieu, quelle géante* you are."

Siobhan laughed. "And did you want us all to be an elf like you?"

"*Mais non, chèrie*, just normal," she minced forward on her high heels. "Ah, and who is this charming creature?"

"My sister Maura. She is engaged to Hugh Prentice and he wants her to have a new outfit for a party Saturday evening. Would you have something for her?"

"*Mais oui*, but of course. She is darker than you, *chèrie*. I will dress her in pale mauve satin. She will be exquisite. It will cost the sweet Hugh much money." Chouchou laughed as she shook Maura's hand and studied her horrified face. "Do not worry, my cabbage. Hugh Prentice is one rich man."

Maura was whirled from one person to the other, swatches of material pinned to her, her hair swept up, pulled back, her chin gripped and turned this way and that. "I feel like I'm being taken apart," she whispered to Siobhan as she slipped on a pair of calf shoes dyed mauve. A dress was dropped over her head and twitched into place by several hands. Maura stared at the person in the mirror, at the tight satin floor-length dress, with its slit up the front, the mauve color turning her hair to deepest mahogany. She was silent.

"You are one gorgeous creature, sister mine," Siobhan muttered.

"I am, aren't I?" Slowly, Maura's smile appeared. "I can't wait for Hughy to see me like this."

"Come with me, *madam*." A less starchy woman than the one who had greeted them, but also dressed in black, spoke to Maura. "Your hair must be dealt with, then your accessories. . . ."

Maura looked alarmed.

"Don't worry... you'll be right upstairs. I'll be along after I speak to Chouchou." Siobhan assured her.

She went along the hall to the small workroom that Chouchou had as her own sanctum sanctorum, knocked once and entered.

The birdlike woman looked up from the dress form layered with material and smiled at her. "So, *chère géant*, you have something on your mind, *hein*?"

"Yes," Siobhan smiled back. "Do you remember the outfit I commented on when I was here for the 'Midnight' creation? The purple silk with the barefoot look, the harem bells on the feet and the jewels between the toes?"

"'Seraglio'!" Chouchou snapped her fingers, then went to the console on her desk, pressed a button, said something in rapid French and returned to her client. "So who is it that you are going to shock, *chèrie*?"

Siobhan shook her head. "I won't tell you, or you might not let me take the outfit." She swung around when the door opened and an attendant appeared with a fall of purple silk draped over one arm, and slippers consisting of a single thong of purple leather to fit between the big toe and the second toe and an ankle thong. When the slippers were on, it looked as though the wearer were barefoot. In the same hand from which the thongs dangled was a box that Siobhan knew would contain the rest of the accessories for the outfit called "Seraglio."

"Here you are, *chèrie*. Try it on behind that screen there and we will see how it goes, *hein*?" Chouchou stated, a glitter deep in those black shoe-button eyes.

It didn't take long to don the one-piece garment that had a gold clasp at one shoulder, then fell like a skintight illusion to the top of her ankles, a short train pulling the tight folds to the back. Siobhan had to take off her stockings to wear the thong slippers, her long slender feet showing to advantage below the tight silk.

She walked out to face Chouchou, arms curved up at her sides, her chin up, her hips forward.

"*Très bien, chèrie*. . .but the gold clasp must go. I shall make you a purple silk pompom for your shoulder. Your hair shall be pushed behind your ears to drape down your back from the crown of your head. No jewelry!" Chouchou rubbed her hands together like a mad scientist. "Except on your toes. There you will wear two amethysts and one gold bell on one foot only. The other shall be bare. *Chèrie*, you will be a goddess! You are so tall, anyway." Chouchou spoke into her console and in minutes, the hairdresser called Jules who did all Chouchou's mannequins was staring at Siobhan, listening to Madame, and clutching his chin.

"Yes, yes, Chouchou. Her makeup must be flawless— a hint of lavender in the base and lip gloss and eye shadow. It must be stark and wild."

As they waxed poetic, Siobhan began to regret her decision to wear something so dramatic. "It might be a cold evening. . ." she began. Her words died in her throat at the looks they gave her.

That evening, she went home with the dress box under her arm and Maura's chatter in her ears.

The few days until Saturday, Maura was so nervous about meeting her future in-laws that she didn't notice how agitated her sister was becoming.

By Saturday morning, Siobhan was convinced that she could find some excuse not to go to a party where Jake Deerfield would announce his engagement.

"I hope she's short and fat with a long aristocratic nose," she mumbled, pressing her face onto her folded arms as she sat in front of the dresser. "I cannot watch him kiss a woman and declare his devotion. I would be sick all over the floor."

"Why aren't you dressed?" Maura's voice quavered. "Lance and Hughy will be down here in twenty minutes to pick us up."

"I have a headache. I think I'll stay here..." Siobhan began, then watched her sister's face collapse.

"You'd make me face them alone?" Maura choked.

"But, honey, you have Hughy and Lance...."

"I need you, sis," Maura gulped.

Siobhan inhaled. "My headache's gone. I'll get dressed."

She hardly paid attention as she dressed, her hands in mechanical obedience to the remembered instructions of Chouchou and Jules. When she went out into the other room, Lance and Hughy were waiting with Maura.

"Cripers!" Lance breathed.

"Love, you'll blow their minds," Hughy chuckled.

"You are so beautiful." Maura came up to her and kissed her cheek. "Shall I show you what was in the flowers that Hughy gave me?" Maura held out her finger. A round glittering diamond held the place of honor on her left hand.

Siobhan kissed her sister, then Hughy, feeling full of love for both of them. "Could we take time for one toast? I have a little New York champagne."

Not waiting for the protest she could see forming on Hughy's lips, Siobhan gestured to Lance to follow her and get the glasses.

They finished the bottle of champagne, toasting themselves and all the people at the party.

"I'd love to keep saluting all these people—" Hughy finally held up the empty bottle "—but we are late."

Unable to think of any more ploys, she picked up a

crocheted wrap, feeling as if she were going to her own hanging.

Maura and Lance went out together, laughing. As Siobhan passed Hughy he leaned toward her. "Your eyes look like dewy violets, my love, and in that outfit, you are going to set many of the First Families on their aristocratic asses."

"Derrières, darling, derrières . . ." Siobhan breathed, her nose in the air, hoping that Hughy couldn't see through her facade to her soggy-oatmeal innards.

The ride to Long Island was a study in contrasts. When they left the apartment building, Manhattan was shrouded in drizzly rain. As they tooled along the highway, the night sky cleared as though some giant janitor had swept the clouds away. The stars came out like faraway flashbulbs on a bed of black velvet, a slice of moon appearing low in the sky and climbing.

"Mmm, smell the night . . ." Maura breathed from the front seat. "So clean."

"Didn't I tell you?" Hughy reached across the seat for her hand, carrying it to his mouth. "I decided to have Manhattan and Long Island hand-laundered especially for you this evening."

"What a sweetiekins you are," Maura cooed, sliding toward her fiancé.

"I may be ill." Lance made a face.

"I heard that . . ." Maura turned around and made a moue at her brother. "Just wait until you fall in love, Lancey boy."

"Don't call me Lancey boy, Maur maur," Lance shot back.

Siobhan was grateful for the laughing argument they had all the way to the Deerfield home. It kept her from thinking. Still, she saw the concerned looks Hughy cast her way in the rearview mirror. She ignored them. She had all she could do to rehearse the way she would act with Jake Deerfield and his intended. Even the thought made her stomach turn sour.

As the car cruised up the circular drive lined with ornately trimmed privets, its enclosed green lawn dotted with flowering shrubs, Siobhan struggled not to bolt from the car and dash down the highway.

"What a fair dinkum house it is!" Lance breathed as he stared around him, then at the attendant who helped the women from the car.

"Many a winter break I spent here," Hughy recalled, a fond look on his face as he came around the front of the car and clasped his fiancée to his side.

"I've changed my mind," Maura muttered. "I don't want to marry you, and I don't want to meet your family."

Hughy held her around the waist as she grabbed for the car door. But the attendant was driving it away. "Too late, my love, you belong to me now. If you don't like my mother and father, then we won't see them. But I'm not giving you up for *any* reason."

"Not see your mother and father!" Maura was stunned. "That's awful. I would never do that to you."

"Thank you." Hughy kissed her nose. "Now come along. I think we're in the way, standing here."

"Yes, let's go inside. Jake said there would be good-lookers here tonight." Siobhan laughed when Lance took her arm with a flourish. "Did I tell you that you look smashing, sis? Is that a dress or trousers or what?" Lance affected a leer.

She pinched his arm. "This is a dress, but it clings around the legs like wraparound trousers. It's a rather wild version of harem pants." She lifted her shawl up over her shoulders.

"Wild is the word." Lance paused on the top step of the broad terrace that fronted on the house. "Lady, you have one great figure, even if you are my sister." He laughed again, then uttered a low whistle as they entered the massive rectangular foyer, with a staircase running up each wall. People moved in and out of large rooms on either side of the foyer.

"Oh, good evening, dear Hugh." A short, plumpish woman came forward, taking hold of Hughy and kissing him on both cheeks. "Your mother and father are in the drawing room, my dear."

"Drawing room?" Lance muttered, bending toward Siobhan. "We're in the middle of an English movie, I think."

"Shhh." Still, she was grateful for Lance's presence. It kept her from thinking about . . . .

"Ah, here you are." Jake's voice reached out, and goose bumps appeared on Siobhan's skin. "Mother, has Hugh been introducing you to his fiancée, Maura, and her brother Lance?"

"Why, yes, Jake he has." His mother turned to face him, just as Jake leaned down and kissed Siobhan's mouth.

Jake lifted his head and smiled at the stunned Siobhan, then took her arm to pull her closer, turning her to face his mother. "This is Siobhan, mother. Darling, this is my mother. Here, let me take your wrap." Jake lifted the shawl from her shoulders, his lips parting as he looked down at her and the dress called "Seraglio."

"My goodness. That dress is—is—quite lovely," Mrs. Deerfield gasped.

For a moment, the five people there were cocooned in

a vibrating silence while Jake and his mother stared at Siobhan.

"He said you were tall," Mrs. Deerfield squeaked, blinking her eyes.

"Yes, I did say that," Jake drawled, his head to one side as his eyes roved her from head to foot. "I had better arm myself with a club tonight, I think."

Siobhan looked from mother to son and back again, a frisson of panic traveling through her body. She opened her mouth to speak, her throat wrestling the words free of her mouth. "How do you do."

"Polite, isn't she?" Jake asked his mother.

"Well, well, Jess. Neglecting your guests, are you?" A more compact version of Jake came up to them, his eyes going to each person, then riveting on Siobhan.

"David." Jessamyn Deerfield blinked, then rallied and introduced everyone but Siobhan to her husband. She tried to take David's arm and lead him away. "Come dear, we must take Hugh to his parents."

"I think Hughy will recognize his family without my help," he answered his wife testily, then looked at Siobhan, his lips pursed. "And who are you?"

"He might not," Jessamyn pursued, tugging at his arm. "Vi is wearing pink tonight. She never wears that color. Hughy could be fooled, couldn't you, dear?"

"Easily." Hughy responded gallantly, earning a contemptuous glower from David Deerfield.

"I repeat, who are you?" He looked at Siobhan, then at Jake, whose arm was around her waist.

"This is Siobhan, father," Jake said, his mouth to Siobhan's temple.

"This is Siobhan?" David repeated, his eyebrows arching.

"David, remember your blood pressure," Jessamyn muttered.

"My blood pressure is that of a twenty-year-old, Jess, as you damn well know." David gave his wife an irritated look.

"Not after tonight," she tittered.

"So, you're the . . ." David Deerfield pronounced each syllable.

"Siobhan wants to dance." Jake whisked her past his parents and out through a large room where, one after another, people lifted their glasses to him and called "Congratulations."

"Shouldn't you be with your fiancée?" a puzzled Siobhan said through her teeth, trying to pry his fingers from her arm and smile at all the grinning faces that greeted them.

"You would think so, but the announcement won't be for a while, so I'll wait until then." Jake whirled her onto the floor despite her struggles to free herself.

"Of all the callous, unfeeling, hypocritical—" She huffed, running out of words as Jake spun her around his body to a disco beat.

"Woman," he stared down at her as she gyrated in front of him, their bodies not quite touching. "I have never seen such a sexy outfit in my life. It would be banned in Boston."

"Stop it." Siobhan looked around her to see if there was an avenue of escape. It startled her to notice that they seemed to be surrounded by people applauding. "Do you realize how embarrassed your fiancée will be?" she hissed.

"Don't sweat it," Jake answered absently, his eyes fixed on her, like magnets to steel.

"Do I get to dance with the bride-to-be, Jake?" someone called from the sidelines.

"Not on your life," Jake laughed back, taking hold of Siobhan at the waist.

When the music ended, they were hemmed in by people.

Siobhan smiled, nodded, oohed, aahed, and found much of the conversation puzzling. She tried edging away from Jake. His hand fastened on her like a staple. "I'd like to go to the powder room," she hissed at him, flashing her smile at a woman who came close to her side.

"What an unusual name you have...Siobhan. Is it a Celtic name?" The woman's unblinking eyes reminded her of a bird watching a worm.

"Yes. It's a Gaelic name. Could you show me where the powder room is?"

"My, my. Fancy you not knowing where things are in your own..."

Jake took hold of her arm and pushed her through the throng of people. "Come along, darling, I'll show you."

"Stop pulling me...." Siobhan tried to wriggle free without drawing too much attention to herself. "And who is that strange woman who was staring at me?"

"That is Florence Basten, the gossip columnist on the *Times*." Jake towed her out into the hall again past a small cluster of older people with his parents at its center. "Father. Mother." Jake acknowledged. "Siobhan wants to use the bathroom."

"Oh, that's perfectly permissible," his mother responded bright-eyed.

"Can't you shut your mouth for a moment and just direct me, instead of trolling me after you like—like a dory." She wanted to close her eyes and wish herself back to her apartment, especially after she heard a wide-hipped, pop-eyed woman announce in Wagnerian tremolo that "it's so cute that Jake is taking her to the bathroom. So original."

When they reached the second floor up the long curving stairway, she was sure it would be less public. She wanted privacy to tell Jake Deerfield what she thought of him. To her horror, there were more people milling around the upstairs hall. "This is a nuthouse," she muttered, a little out of breath.

"Come along, dearest, we'll go through here." Jake led her through closed doors that he unlocked. "This is the family section of the house. No one else will come this way."

"How nice. The other half of the house is for the visiting lunatics. This is for the resident nuts." She followed him into a very masculine suite done in tan and black. "This must be your apartment. It's so depressing." Siobhan patted at her hair when she caught sight of herself in the mirror and glimpsed the tight hurt look on Jake's face. Then it was gone. She whirled to face him. "That was uncalled for, and bitchy. I apologize. It's just that I didn't want to come this evening."

"You made that plain." Jake spoke in neutral tones. "The bathroom is this way." He gestured down a short hall off the bedroom.

"Thank you." Siobhan went into the tan and beige bathroom, closing the door and leaning back against it with her eyes closed. "How am I going to last the evening?" she quizzed herself, then sighed and pushed herself away from the door, used the facilities and freshened her makeup. She washed her hands for the second time and dawdled until she was sure that Jake had rejoined the party. Then she left the bathroom and returned to the bedroom.

"I thought I might have to break down the door,"

Jake said from the huge square bed, covered in tan satin, his head propped against the console at the head, his shod feet casually spread on the satin. "Come here."

"No. Time to go downstairs." Siobhan eyed the distance she would have to travel to the door.

"You wouldn't make it, darling. I'd get you first and drag you back. Now, do you come here and talk to me for a moment? Or do I come and get you?"

"Are you so insensitive that you don't care what your fiancée would say? By the way, what's her name, anyway?" She moved closer and looked down at Jake lying on the bed.

He sat up and reached for her in one fluid motion, drawing her forward and down on his body. "There. Isn't that better?" he grinned down at her.

"No. Will you let me get up?" Siobhan could feel the bodice of her dress being dragged down. She desperately tried with one hand to hold it in place.

"I don't mind if your dress comes down in front, love," Jake crooned, his hand stilling hers as his mouth came down on the expanse of skin above her breasts.

"Jake, have you no shame? At least if you don't care about me...."

"I care about you a great deal, and I think about you too damn much for my own good. My work is suffering."

"And what is your work, Machiavelli?" she jeered trying to stretch her body away from him and succeeding only in showing him more flesh.

"Darling...you know what I do. I'm in computers. My business includes a few television stations...."

"A few television stations! Like a few tomatoes, maybe...." Siobhan wriggled. "Let me go."

"Not yet." Jake held her against his body, cradling her

he sat back once more. "I produce movies. I own a computer company in California. I own a Formula One racing car, though I don't race anymore . . . ."

"I don't want to hear." Siobhan stopped struggling and looked up at him. "You mean that you used to race those horrid machines that go hundreds of miles an hour?"

Jake nodded, kissing her nose. "I also own a sheep station in Australia which—"

"You risked your life in that foolish fashion?" Siobhan wanted to tear the smile from his face. "How dare you do something so stupid?" She felt as though she were frothing at the mouth. She had to swallow twice before her throat cleared.

"I love the way your breasts move when you're upset." Jake leaned down to kiss her.

Siobhan pushed his head away.

A knock at the door was followed by Jake's mother's voice calling to him.

"Come in, mother," Jake responded.

Pushing at Jake to free her, Siobhan half slid off the bed as Mrs. Deerfield entered.

"Oh," his mother said staring at Siobhan, who was now sitting on the floor. "I didn't know you were busy."

"We were just finishing," Jake assured her.

"How could you?" Siobhan seethed, "Mrs. Deerfield, I can explain."

"Oh, no need, my dear, I fully understand. Mr. Deerfield and I were quite as involved with each other when we were young. Of course, I don't think we were quite as acrobatic." She smiled blindly at Siobhan, then looked at her son, who was now on his feet at the opposite side of the bed. "Dear, I think your father would like to make the announcement now. Do you think you might come downstairs and continue this later—" She smiled when her son nodded, and then bustled out the door.

"Well, that's the limit," Siobhan huffed, going to the mirror to repair her makeup with a shaking hand. "I have never been in such an amoral household. How could your mother countenance you being up here with me?"

"Oh, mother stopped dictating my behavior years ago," Jake assured her, staring at her reflection in the mirror. "You do look so beautiful tonight, darling, like a lovely orchid. Your eyes, that dress, all a beautiful purple color. Listen to me, I sound more like a botanist..." He kissed her bare shoulder, "...than your lover."

Siobhan jumped at the word as though she were stung. "You are not—" She shook her head at him, wiped her shaking mouth and drew a deep breath.

"I think we'd better hurry, angel," Jake said to her.

"Why don't you go ahead?"

"No, I'm waiting for you." Jake's tight-lipped look told her he wouldn't budge.

Shrugging, she gave a last twitch to her skirt and turned toward him.

"I am not going to let anyone else dance with you. They might step on your lovely feet." He looked down at her toes, smiled, then gazed into her eyes again. "I think I would like taking those jewels off your toes with my teeth."

"Jake, let's go." She stalked toward the door, wishing she weren't so inhibited in her movements by the garment she wore.

He caught up with her in the hall, before she reached the double doors leading to the section of the house open to guests.

To Siobhan's surprise, there didn't seem to be anyone in sight. She assumed they had gone down to dance or drink.

As she and Jake descended the stairs, many eyes looked upward, and it seemed that people in the other rooms were crowding into the huge foyer.

"So, there you are. Come along. We'll go into the solarium. There's more room," David Deerfield called up to them, then he ushered the people around him through the drawing room.

"Ah, yes, the solarium..." Siobhan repeated in syrupy tones. "And is that where we will have the human sacrifice?"

"Something like that," Jake chuckled, not releasing her when they reached the foyer, but shepherding her through the drawing room, most of the guests ahead of them.

When they reached the large, pleasantly steamy room, its three glass walls allowing a panoramic view of the grounds, the crowd parted like the Red Sea to let them proceed.

"I will wait back here. I want to look for Lance and Maura and Hughy," Siobhan muttered.

"Not to worry. Maura and Hughy are up near the musicians' podium, standing with his parents and mine. See? Ah, there's Lance talking to the young Chisholm girl."

"I'd still rather stay back here." She tried to dig in her heels.

To Siobhan's shock Jake grinned and then swept her up into his arms and walked easily to the other side of the room. Siobhan was too stunned to say anything, the sounds of the laughter around them making the blood rise to her face. "For heaven's sake," she gasped as she was dumped back on her feet in front of his mother.

"Goodness, James Kendall, you are even more impetuous than your father!"

"Could we get on with this?" David Deerfield growled, signaling to the drummer to give him a roll on his instruments. Then he stood up on the podium, fiddled with a microphone and began to speak, his voice reverberating around the room. "Ladies and gentlemen, friends...as you know we are gathered here this evening for a very special announcement, my son's engagement. But Vi and Herb Prentice have decided to horn in on the show. Since the parents of the girls are in Australia, we, as parents of the men are going to do the announcing...."

"David, you are rambling, as usual," Herb Prentice said, standing up next to his friend. "To make this concise: the Prentices and the Deerfields announce the engagements or betrothals, whichever you prefer, to the Butler girls, Maura to my son Hugh and Siobhan to their son Jake."

The cheers rang in her ears, like discordant church bells. For long moments she thought she would faint as smiling faces went in and out of her vision. When Jake leaned over her and kissed her, she was limp in his arms.

"You're mine forever, as you have been since the moment we met," he muttered in her ear.

"You're out of your mind," Siobhan babbled. "Where is your fiancée?"

"You're it, my darling." Jake turned to acknowledge a congratulation, but his arm tightened when she sagged against him.

"Darling, isn't it wonderful!" A flushed, bright eyed Maura came up to her. "Isn't it too bad that you couldn't have a ring, too."

"Not to worry, Maura. This is for her. It was my

grandmother's ring." Jake flashed a marquise-shaped emerald, then slipped it onto Siobhan's finger.

"No," she protested, as people grabbed her hand to shake it, or kissed her on the cheek.

"When are you being married?" Mrs. Prentice came up to Siobhan. "Hughy and Maura want a summer wedding."

"Never."

"In three weeks." Jake's voice overrode hers.

Hot lava filled Siobhan, her veins and arteries on fire as she turned to face Jake. "Not on your aristocratic backside, brother." Yanking her hand free, she strode blindly through the crowds, mumbling her pardon as she bounced into several people in her hurry to get up the stairs to a more private place.

"Siobhan! Siobhan! Come this way," Jessamyn Deerfield called, slightly out of breath from trying to catch up to her. She pointed down a hallway, unlocked a set of double doors, then gestured for Siobhan to precede her.

Neither of them spoke until they entered a corner room, done in pink and cream and clearly a woman's sitting room.

"This is my hideout," Jessamyn said simply. "I love that husband of mine, but sometimes he's too much for me. He's a rocket person in a fast-lane life, and when he comes home he blasts my ordered existence apart." Jessamyn watched Siobhan, the smile flitting across her face not quite hiding her anxious look. "Jake and his father can be like tractor trailers at times—they roll you flat and never realize it." Jessamyn licked her lips and clasped her hands in front of her as she sat on the mauve satin love seat across from Siobhan. "What did Jake do to you?"

"Now? Yesterday? Or years ago?" Siobhan pushed the words from her tight throat.

Jessamyn unclasped her hands, her eyes narrowing. "He hurt you very much. Could he have hurt you so if you didn't care for him?"

Siobhan's head shot up. "Would you care for a man who used you for a one-night stand?" She sucked in a breath, shocked that she had said such a thing to Jake's mother.

Mrs. Deerfield stared at her. "So—you came out here, dressed to kill in that gorgeous outfit, ready to face what you thought was going to be another woman."

"I do care for Jake, but—" Siobhan fumbled.

"I think I'd like you as a daughter-in-law. And I would like you to help me do something."

"What do you mean?" Siobhan quizzed the older woman.

"I would not be unhappy to see my arrogant son hoist with his own petard, as they say."

6

SIOBHAN BLINKED at Jake's mother, a petite woman with an impish look about her. "Mrs. Deerfield—"

"Do call me Jess, dear. If we are going to be coplotters."

"I don't think I quite understand."

"I have a few scores to settle with the men in the Deerfield family, child. It's not that they are chauvinistic—I have always had shares and a say in the business." Jess looked out the window, her own reflection staring back at her. "It's just that sometimes they ride roughshod over feelings, assuming that we, their women, will understand that they are just being men. I understand, all right, but I often wonder if the same understanding would be coming my way if I treated David in such a cavalier fashion." A bemused look crossed her face. "What a golden opportunity to show my men the other facets of me!"

"That women are chameleons—changing and growing." Siobhan recalled how Jake had mocked her hair color when they first met.

"That we're not just what we seem, that we evolve and broaden..." Mrs. Deerfield patted her hips. "Other than in the literal sense, of course."

Siobhan laughed, feeling some of the stricture around her heart loosen. "Jake thought I was a hopeless case when he first met me—that I would never be any dif-

ferent than the harried waitress I was when we met."
She smiled at his mother, trying to mask her pain as she
spoke.

"Cretin," Jess said through pursed lips. "Well? What
do you say? Shall we give them a bit of a run?"

"We? Are you sure...?"

"The more I hear you talk, the more I see my David.
We shall begin by having a few get-togethers in New
York, I think."

The sharp raps on the door startled both women.

"Mother, mother is Siobhan there with you?" Jake's
voice was a well modulated roar.

Siobhan bristled at the tone, then turned to look at his
grinning mother.

"Siobhan, my child, you could run from him now,
but he would only come looking for you. Why not teach
him a few things? Then, if you must, dump him! You'll
feel better for it."

"It would be a terrible thing to do," Siobhan whispered back.

"So?"

"Siobhan? Siobhan, damn you, answer me," Jake bellowed, rattling the knob so hard, the frame of the door
shook.

"Let's do it," she suddenly decided looking at the
door. She felt a wild elation that now she wouldn't have
to leave Jake at once. Being with him would still be a
two-edged sword, however. Each day she would love
him more, but each day could bring her closer to leaving
him for good.

"Do stop banging on the door, dear. I'm getting a
headache," his mother called, then winked at her co-
conspirator as she unlocked it. She was almost flattened
against the wall, as Jake plunged through the entrance,

his eyes searching for and at once finding his intended.

Siobhan rose to her feet, her eyes flicking once to his mother then back to Jake. Back straight, chin up, calm, she faced him, allowing a small smile as he strode toward her. "Shouldn't you apologize to your mother for almost slamming her into the wall?" It took all her training as an actress not to flinch at the hot menace in his face.

"What?" He wheeled around to face his diminutive parent, still standing against the wall. "Oh. Sorry, mother. I was trying to get in."

"So we deduced, James Kendall," his mother said sweetly. "You'll be right down, won't you Siobhan?"

"Yes of course, Jess." she answered, in just as syrupy a voice.

Jake stared at his mother, his eyes assessing, as she left the room and closed the door. His eyes were just as watchful as he turned back to gaze at Siobhan. "What's been going on?"

"Not a thing. Your mother felt she should try to get to know me better since I will be her daughter in—" she looked at him inquiringly—"how many weeks?"

"Three," Jake growled, a restless scrutiny in his look. "And you needn't try to get away to Australia either."

"Perhaps you could take me there on our wedding trip. Will we have a honeymoon, do you think?"

"Oh, I think so." Jake's nostrils flared as though he were testing the atmosphere for aliens, wariness in every line of his body.

"Shall we join the others downstairs? I'm sure there will be friends who will want to see my ring."

Jake leaned over her, inhaling her perfume, his mouth at her temple. "There you go changing on me again. We could stay up here for a while. Tonight you'll be sleeping with me."

"No!" Siobhan snapped. Then her eyes slid away from him. "This is your parents' home."

"I'm aware of that." Jake's eyes narrowed on her.

"Maura's at my apartment." She pressed her lips together.

"She can sleep at Hughy's," Jake stated. "Are you saying that we shouldn't sleep together until we're married?"

She was about to tell him where he could go when she remembered his mother. *I'm an actress, aren't I*, she asked herself. She took deep breaths and thought of peeling onions, bringing tears to her eyes.

"What's going on?" Jake straightened from his lounging stance, grasping her chin with one hand. "You aren't a crier," he mused, his eyes piercing her.

"You're right. I never cry." She hiccuped, smothering the voice that reminded her that she had never needed false crutches, that she was a free spirit.

All at once it became appealing—paying Jake back, not with knife thrusts, but with needle jabs. She would excise her own burning scars this way.

She draped herself over his arm. "Shall we join the others?"

"Changing again," Jake mumbled, his hand closing over hers as it lay on his arm.

Down on the main floor, Lance came forward and claimed her for a dance, Jake releasing her reluctantly.

They had almost circled the floor before Lance spoke to her. "Why are you acting so strange, sis? Draping yourself over Jake that way!"

"Don't worry about it," Siobhan said testily.

"I like Jake and his family," Lance told her.

"Good for you," she made a face at him.

When she danced with Hughy a few moments later,

he frowned at her. "Listen, love. Whatever you're planning about Jake—and don't bother denying that you are—count me out. I saw you come downstairs right after Jess, who couldn't keep the cat that ate the goldfish grin off her face." Hughy leaned back a bit and looked down at her. "Child, didn't you know that people die in an explosion? And that's what will happen if Jake finds out you're playing games with him."

"You must have had too much champagne, Hughy dear."

He sighed. "I tried—and that's what I'll mention when I give your eulogy."

"Ghoul."

"May I cut in?" Jake's lips barely parted on the words, the cobra look he threw at Hughy making Siobhan wince. Hughy shrugged and walked away. "What was he saying to you?"

"Oh, Hughy was telling me how the part at Zenith is tailor-made for me," she simpered.

"Does he often repeat himself that way? You told me he told you that a while ago." Jake speared her with those midnight-blue eyes.

"He is a bit young for senility," Siobhan ventured, smiling, her mind going into high gear.

"What are you thinking, Siobhan?"

"Ah...I can't make up my mind what to wear to the dance at the Club next week." She sighed, hoping her agitation looked like dejection. If she had to spar with him like this for three more weeks, she'd be a wreck.

"Since when have you been so worried about clothes." He nibbled at her ear lobe. "Food. Yes, you were always interested in food."

"Darling, my image." Siobhan sagged against him, wondering if that was a flicker of amusement deep in his eyes. He would end up hating her for acting like this. *Isn't that the idea*, a voice deep inside reminded her. Better he should hate her now, than in two or three years when he tired of her.

"Sweetie, have you been into the champagne?"

"Just a teensy smidgeon," she admitted.

"Teensy smidgeon! When did you start talking like a Barbie doll?" His face closed as his eyes went over her.

Siobhan looked around the room, spotted Jake's father passing by, and corralled him. "Isn't this our dance?"

David Deerfield looked from Siobhan to his grim-faced son, smiled and nodded.

Keeping the plastic smile pinned to her lips, she tried to follow David's giant steps as he led her around the floor. "What's going on here? Or shouldn't I ask?"

"I'm not sure I know myself," Siobhan sighed.

He stared down at her, then smiled. "Jess and I had a few battles in our time."

"I'll bet we could top you," she mumbled.

"Jake and Hughy have said that you are a very good actress."

Her head jerked up as she stared at the bland expression on David's face. "Thank you. I like acting."

"Everyone should like what they do." He whirled her around the floor, Siobhan's feet sometimes leaving the ground.

"True," she panted, squeezing her eyes shut as they seemed headed for a potted plant at the side of the dance floor. Somehow they missed it, but she sighed with relief when the music stopped.

"May I have my lady back now?" Jake looked down at her, a glint in his eyes. He swept her close to his side, exchanged a few pleasantries with his father, nodded to a few friends, then took her in his arms. "I can see that you are never going to bore me," he muttered in her ear.

"What does that mean?" She measured the distance to the door.

"Nothing, darling," Jake crooned, his mouth brushing her ear. "What could it mean, except that sometimes I forget how changeable you are."

"Why do you say that?" she whispered.

"You're trembling, love." Jake ignored her question. "Why?"

"Maybe I'm cold?"

"I don't think so."

"Getting late," Siobhan gulped, feeling like a butterfly tacked to a board as Jake continued to gaze at her, a half smile on his face. A strong survival instinct, honed by years of being on her own, made her sense the change in Jake—an awareness of danger that made her skin prickle. Could he know what she and his mother had discussed?

"I want to talk to your mother," Jake nuzzled her hair. "I'll call her from the office on Monday and tell her about our engagement."

"No hurry," she gulped. "I'll write her."

"Darling, what's bothering you?" His silken amusement made her goose bumps swell to egg size.

"Nothing." Siobhan reached out a hand and grabbed Maura's arm as she danced by with Hughy, shaking the girl out of her dreamy reverie. "Time to go. I'm tired," she told her surprised sister.

"Vona," Maura moaned. "You can't mean it. I'm having such a good time. I just love Hughy's family, and we're all going to breakfast at his house," Maura babbled, her body draped over Hughy's.

"Take that silly smile off your face, Hughy." Siobhan said tartly, determined that someone should be sensible and help her skip the country—to Zimbabwe, perhaps. *But Jake can't be fooled,* her mind screamed.

"Can't," Hughy beamed at her. "And Lance won't want to go either. He's starting his own harem over there."

"Don't be disgusting," Siobhan pinched his arm and rolled her eyes toward Jake. *Help!* she begged Hughy silently.

"Have you got a tic in your eye, sis?" Maura asked, concerned.

"No," Jake turned toward Siobhan, kissing her on the cheek. "She's trying to get Hughy to take her back to Manhattan. I should have told her she was staying here until Sunday, and that you will be staying with the Prentices." Jake smiled at an ecstatic Maura.

"Is that what we're doing, Hughy? What a marvelous idea! Do you think your parents will mind?"

"No, my love, they'll be delighted to keep you under their roof permanently," Hughy responded.

"Really, Maura," Siobhan looked from one to the other. "What about Lance." They looked at her blankly.

"He's staying here, darling, as you are. He is really having a wonderful time," Jake informed her, taking her chin and turning it so that she could glimpse her little brother holding forth in front of goggle-eyed debutantes.

"I've got no clothes," she whispered, seeking a rescue from Jake's web.

"Not to worry." Jake kissed her mouth. "Chouchou sent clothes for you."

"I'm not a kept woman," she squeaked, watching Hughy dance away with Maura.

"No, certainly not. I'm a kept man. Yours."

As she looked up at him, pain and indecision coursed

through her veins. "I don't understand you," she gulped, hope and despair rioting in her.

"I know," he soothed. "You never have. We had a bad beginning, but all that will be straightened out now."

"It will?"

"Yes. Shall we dance, love? It's the only way I can hold you in front of all these people. And I want to hold you."

"I think I should talk to your mother," she gasped when his hand settled feather light on her derriere. "It's not polite to ignore her."

"You talked to her for almost an hour," Jake spoke into her hair. "You should spend time with me now."

"Right." Siobhan capitulated with a groan of delight when Jake's questing hand slid up under her breast. "I don't know what I'm going to do," she mumbled to herself, her mind like cotton candy.

"Don't worry about anything. I'll take care of you."

"No," Her eyes closed as she and Jake swayed together. "I want to take care of myself. It's not wise to depend on anyone."

"All right, love, if that's the way you want it. You take care of me. I'd love that."

"You'd hate it," she contradicted him.

Jake leaned back from her. "I'd give everything I own if I could wipe away the moments when we first met." His smile gave her tremors. "It accomplished one thing. I have never been drunk since—or lashed out at anyone in a hangover temper."

"No?"

"No."

"That's good," Siobhan breathed, closing her eyes and letting her body relax.

"Trust me, darling."

Siobhan stiffened. How many times had she heard that from men who dated her?

"Siobhan? Siobhan, what is it?"

"Nothing." *What would you think, James Kendall Deerfield, if I told you that I almost let down my guard? That I almost believed what you said?*

She forced her mind to concentrate on her defense mechanisms because her body wanted to succumb to Jake Deerfield, her spirit wanted to give itself to him. Her mind fought back, remembered the pain, recalled the drudgery of working and going to school, of eating one meal a day and supplementing it with water.

Siobhan was grateful to the people who crowded around them and wanted to dance with her. She felt shy and unsure of herself with the many uncles and cousins who claimed her for a turn around the floor.

"Jake was always the luckiest in the family," Cousin Richard informed her. "He stood to inherit the most money, so what does he do? He decides that he'll branch off on his own and found his own company. He goes into computers and—boom! He couldn't handle all the business. Then television, then movies. But you know all that, don't you? What woman wouldn't want to be married to a man like Jake?" Richard looked down at her through horn-rimmed glasses. "There are lots of women who would love to step into your shoes."

"I wear a nine triple A with four A heel. I hope they all have narrow feet." Siobhan showed her teeth in the smile.

"Ha, ha! I like a woman with a sense of humor," Richard nodded.

"How astute of you to recognize it," Siobhan beamed.

He stared at her for a moment. "I've offended you."

He sighed. "That does it. Jake will break both my arms."

She laughed. "He won't do that."

"Jake is good-natured about most things, and he doesn't give a damn about money. He's made and lost a few fortunes in his time and wouldn't balk at having to start over with nothing but a dime in his pocket. But he isn't the same about you. He has the family shaking in its shoes—"

Siobhan stopped dancing and stared up at him, open-mouthed.

Before she could ask Richard to explain himself, she was whirled away by Cousin Marshall, who waltzed like a gamecock out of control.

At last, when she was quite sure her feet would be permanently numb, she found a corner, sent one of the cousins for a cool drink and sat down in the nearest chair.

"Ah, there you are, dear. I have been trying to get you away from Jake for a few moments," Jessamyn began.

"He knows," Siobhan gasped.

His mother stared at her for a few moments, then gave herself a little shake and smiled. "My dear, you must take that hunted look off your face. Otherwise David and Jake will guess what we are doing."

Siobhan looked at her smiling mother-in-law-to-be and closed her eyes. "This is not going to work. I think we should abandon the whole idea and I'll just disappear to China. He'd never think to look for me there."

"Tut, tut, child," Mrs. Deerfield nodded her thanks to the attendant who appeared with a chair for her. "You must have more spirit about this, more courage. Think of the challenge—putting something over on the Deerfield men." She sighed, a benign smile on her face. "You wouldn't deny a person something that would make them happy to their dying day, would you?"

"No, but I don't believe that Jake can be fooled." Siobhan took a drink from the tray of a passing waiter, then coughed on a long swallow of whiskey.

"Of course, if you are going to imbibe heavily, it would imperil our chances of success." Mrs. Deerfield frowned at Siobhan's reddened face.

"Not a drinker." Siobhan coughed.

"Everyone with problems says that, dear. The best thing is to quit cold turkey, as they say," Jake's mother informed her.

"Right," Siobhan agreed, and put her glass on a table beside her. "Perhaps if I switched to Saratoga water and lime?"

"Excellent." Jessamyn signaled another waiter and gave the order for two Saratoga water drinks with lime. "Now, where were we? Ah, yes, you were saying that Jake knows. . . ."

"Maybe he doesn't know everything, but he senses something." Siobhan stumbled through an explanation. "He wasn't angry with me any more. He smiled at me."

"He would do that, dear. He loves you." Jess smiled at the waiter and handed Siobhan one of the glasses. "You mustn't worry about anything. I am so glad that you insisted on staying the night."

"I insisted?"

"Yes. . . Jake and Maura said that you were dying to sleep in your new quarters."

"New quarters?" Siobhan could feel her eyes widening.

"Must you repeat everything I say, dear?" Jess said, then becoming contrite. "Unless, of course, you have a hearing problem. Oh dear, Jake didn't tell us that—not that it makes any difference in the way we feel about you, because it doesn't." Jess raised her voice, making a few heads turn toward them. "I shall tell the staff to speak more plainly—"

"Jess, what in heaven's name are you shouting about?" David came up to them. "The Wendells are leaving."

"Speak up, David, please." Jess sounded out every word like a jackhammer on concrete.

"Jess, what has gotten into you" David excused himself to Siobhan and led his shouting wife away.

Siobhan sat there, gulping great breaths of air, shocked beyond measure when her shaking hands found a wetness on her cheeks. "I never cry." She sucked in a shuddering breath.

"Darling, there you are. What's wrong? You never cry and now twice in one evening I find tears on your cheeks. Are you ill?"

"Your mother thinks I am hearing-impaired," Siobhan sobbed.

"Does she?" Jake chuckled and leaned down to pull her up into his arms. "I'm sure she told you it made no difference to the way she felt about you."

"That's what she said." Siobhan hiccuped against Jake's chest, her fingers pulling and tugging at the hand-sewn pleats on his dress shirt.

"See."

"You were born into a circus," she gulped.

"True, but I was happy as a child. My mother freely admitted that she hasn't understood what has driven me since I was five years old."

"Brave woman." Siobhan stroked his cheeks as she tried not to notice the people around them. Although many people had taken their leave, there were still a great many remaining.

Jessamyn Deerfield returned to their side. "I should have taken you with me to wish them good night, dear." She shrugged. "We won't worry about it since there are so many others here." Then she frowned. "I do hope Frances has pressed your jodhpurs, dear; you'll need them for your morning ride."

"I don't ride that well, Jess."

Jake's mother looked surprised. "Really? You mustn't be so modest, dear. When Jake had that lovely filly delivered here the other day for you, I assumed you must be a top-drawer rider."

"Horse? For me?"

"Of course for you. You didn't have a horse to ride, did you?"

"Ah—no, but . . . ."

"Now you do, dear. The sweetest bay filly I have seen in ever so long, isn't that right, David?"

"Yes, she is a beauty. Now you'll be able to ride whenever you choose, Siobhan."

"Terrific," she whispered, her eyes sliding toward Jake who was biting his lip.

"Darling, you'll love her," he told her, slipping his arm around her waist.

"Why did you let your parents think that I rode?" she fumed as soon as the others had drifted off.

"I didn't, love. Come, this way, we have to say good night to our guests."

"Then how did they get the idea? Oh, thank you, yes, it has been an exciting weekend. Ah, well, maybe we won't be getting married in three weeks. . . ."

"Sweetheart, how you talk," Jake squeezed her to his

side. "Mrs. Taylor will think you don't want to marry me."

"How odd." Siobhan smiled until her face hurt and she was ready to collapse when the last straggler left. "It's bed for me."

"Oh, my dear, not yet!' Viola Prentice flapped her hand at Siobhan. "We are having breakfast at Dandelion Hill."

"Is there really such a place?" Siobhan quizzed Jake.

"I heard that," Hughy came up behind her. "I'll have you know that Dandelion Hill is the old homestead where I was raised." Hughy looked at his friend critically. "You look as though someone performed a lobotomy on you, love. Tough evening?"

"Drop dead Hughy Prentice," she said through her teeth.

Siobhan glumly followed her glassy-eyed sister out the front door to the line of waiting limousines. "Don't tell me you have a stable of limousines as well as horses."

"The Prentices ordered the cars, darling," Jake told her. He helped her into the back of chauffeur driven Rolls, followed and took her in his arms.

"Aren't you past the stage of necking in the back seat of a car?" she hissed, looking at the back of the driver's head.

"I thought so. But with you everything is brand-new."

Siobhan's heart jerked out of rhythm at his words. "That was a sweet thing to say." She lifted her hand to his face.

"I intend to spend much of the next eighty years saying sweet things to you. Say some to me." Jake looked down at her, his face still.

Siobhan opened her mouth to tell him he could wait until hell froze over. "I love your dimples," she told him, sighing.

"Woman, I am going to practice doing whatever I have to do to make those dimples, as you call them, appear. I need every hold over you I can muster."

Siobhan stared up at him in the darkness of the car, aware of the murmurs of Hughy and Maura, sitting in front with the driver. "I really don't fit into this party-party scene, Jake, and I don't know if I would want to. It just doesn't seem worthwhile." She waited for the explosion.

"It's true that our life may seem like a merry-go-round at times, and that's because it *is* like that—but not all the time. I, too, like privacy, quiet, dinner à deux. We'll have to make adjustments, compromises. It won't be easy, but I happen to think it's worth the struggle."

"And if we don't win the struggle? If marriage is a drag? What do we do? Throw it away?" Siobhan tried to clear the hoarseness from her voice.

Jake leaned back from her, his arms lifting and crossing behind his neck. "I suppose we do what everyone else does under the circumstance. We'll try a little harder."

"Or junk it," she said sharply.

"Siobhan, lighten up." Jake dropped his arms and crossed them in front of him, gazing out his window at the kaleidoscope of light from passing cars.

The rest of the short ride to Dandelion Hill was devoid of conversation. Siobhan was relieved that Maura and Hughy seemed too involved with each other to notice the silence in the back seat.

Dandelion Hill was on a small incline, a comfortable

brick home that clung to the top of the knoll. She climbed out of the car before Jake, feeling light-headed and disoriented.

Under cover of laughter and talking, Siobhan gravitated to Lance's side. "I'd like to meet your new friends, boyo," she crooned.

He made the introductions, and although she responded, she couldn't remember one name that Lance mentioned. Nor could she have recalled, five minutes after speaking, what she had said to the young girls she met.

She pushed eggs and sausage around her plate and exclaimed with the rest that nothing tasted better in the early morning than coffee. In truth she had to stifle a gag at the breakfast smell.

By the time she was to return with Jake and Lance to the Deerfield home, she was reeling with exhaustion. She was hardly aware of making her farewells to the Prentices, Hughy and Maura.

On the ride back, she pretended to sleep, letting Jake and Lance talk. Mr. and Mrs. Deerfield sat in the front with the hired driver. The other hired cars had already returned to the auto livery.

When Jake would have picked her up and carried her into the house, Siobhan demurred. "No, don't. I'd rather walk. Good night everyone." Her smile slipped over Jake's parents and Lance. Then she was hurrying into the house, intent only on getting to her room and locking the door. She was damn well not going to let Jake into her room.

She hung her dress on a hanger but the rest of her clothes she tossed on a chair. She washed her face and brushed her teeth, then staggered from the bathroom across the bedroom to fall into bed. She fell into sleep as though she had just tumbled from a mountain peak.

THE NEXT day, a maid woke her, proffering a large glass of fresh-squeezed orange juice and a steaming cup of cocoa.

Siobhan's eyes felt as though they had been glued shut. They were sticky and unfocused even when they were open. Rather than argue with the smiling girl, she took the tray from her and set it on a low table in front of the love seat near the window. Bleary-eyed as she was, she couldn't help but admire the lavender, purple and cream decor, with a purple and cream Indian rug on the floor. She swayed in the middle of the bedroom, stretching her arms above her head and yawning. With a little bit of luck and enough dawdling in the shower, she might just miss the early morning horseback ride planned for her by Jake and his family.

Siobhan stared at the enormous bathroom. "This is larger than the locker room at the 'Y,'" she exclaimed to herself, letting her eyes rove over the cream bathroom, admiring the azuelos done in lavender and purple. She could feel the smile lift her mouth as she studied the round sunken tub. "To blazes with the shower," she muttered. "I will soak my shattered being in bubbling water." She switched on the jacuzzi and dropped her robe. When she felt the draft at her back as she took the first step down into the pool, she spoke without turning. "You could tell my brother and Mr. Deerfield to go on without me, Lana. I'm going to soak for a few minutes."

"You forgot your juice and cocoa." The amusement in Jake's voice stiffened her, but still she didn't turn. "I've brought them to you, love."

"Kind of you," she grated, stepping down into the tub

fully and immersing herself, still without looking at Jake.

"It looks very inviting." He set the tray down on the tile area that also acted as a splash back, then he stripped off his shirt.

Siobhan looked at him for the first time. "There isn't room...." It startled her to see how fast he undressed, then she felt the heat in her body as she looked at those strong muscular thighs, narrow hips, broad shoulders and chest, long legs, the dark arrow of hair on his chest the same color as his head, but a little curlier.

"Don't keep looking at me like that, darling. It's very sexy," Jake laughed at her.

Siobhan looked away at once and clutched at the orange-juice glass, draining the cold tart liquid down to the bits of pulp. "Good juice," she gasped, feeling the waves of water over her shoulders as Jake settled himself next to her. "Would you like some of my cocoa?" Her voice was hoarse again.

"Yes." His hand touched her abdomen. "Your skin is soft but firm. I like that."

"Glad to oblige. Here. Have some cocoa." She held the cup out to him.

"Feed me." Jake edged closer to her.

"It'll spill."

"No it won't."

She leaned closer, moving carefully so that she wouldn't spill any of the still-hot liquid. "You have very few fillings," she remarked as she looked into his open mouth, then fitted the cup on his lips.

"See what a good catch I am? Our children will have good teeth like their father."

"Their mother has good teeth too. See." Siobhan opened her mouth, her head back, the index finger of her right hand pulling down her lip. Then she realized what she had said and shot upward to a sitting position in the tub, her face averted.

"Don't look away, my love. It delights me that you're finally coming to accept that you will be the mother of my children." Jake took hold of her chin and turned it back to face him. "You will never get away from me, darling Siobhan, so why not just relax and enjoy our time together."

"It sounds too much like bondage to me," she said through tight lips.

"Call it whatever you like, Siobhan. You are not getting away from me."

THE NEXT morning Jess met her when she came down from her room. "My dear, I am so glad you are an early riser." She flung her arm out, pointing down the long hall. "The enemy are in the morning room, wolfing down prodigious amounts of food." She blinked. "How can they do that?"

Siobhan laughed, then hiccuped.

"My dear, what is it?" Jess looked at her wide-eyed.

"I hiccup when I'm nervous. Mrs. Deerfield—"

"Jess, dear. Did you forget?"

"Jess. Ah—I don't think I can fool Jake."

"Tut, tut, child. Faint heart and all that rot." Jess took her arm and led her down the hall. "It's not as if we want to hurt them—just bend them a little." Her gamine grin made Siobhan laugh but didn't lessen her trepidation.

"What are we doing?" she whispered as they approached the morning room. She could hear the rustle of someone reading a newspaper.

"Just follow my lead, dear, and don't worry. When in doubt, cry. You'll see."

The two women walked into the sunny room with window walls that looked out on a terraced garden.

Jake rose to his feet, his narrow-eyed stare taking in her pink suede narrow-legged pants with the peach and pink striped silk blouse. "You look lovely, darling." He came close to her, his arms going around her, his mouth dropping to hers.

"Jake, stop it!" Siobhan gasped.

"Yes, James Kendall, leave her alone. We women don't choose to be mauled," Jess stated, her smile encouraging Siobhan.

"Ah...yes. We women don't..." she faltered and swallowed.

"Damn. Jess, what are you trying to do with Siobhan?" David Deerfield had come around to his wife's chair, kissing her on the top of the head. "And don't bother sputtering at me that you don't know what I'm talking about. You've been filling her head with something, and if you don't watch out, your only son will—"

"Don't be silly," Siobhan coughed to clear the squeak from her voice.

"Darling, don't bother trying to cover up. You aren't good enough at it." Jake drawled. "Mother, do not try to involve Siobhan in anything. We have enough to settle without adding your little intrigues to the lot. Find another way to pay back father and me for being the bastards we are. Don't include Siobhan."

"James Kendall, I have never called you or your father a bastard. I do not use such language," Jess humphed. "Not that the implied insult doesn't fit, you understand. It's just that I am too much of a lady...."

David Deerfield, who was still standing next to his seated wife, bent to kiss her again. "Yes, my darling, we know you are a lady—and that you've put up with thoughtlessness from us. But give your new daughter a chance before you put her in the game plan."

Jess raised her chin even higher. "I have not admitted there was a game plan."

Siobhan stood silent in the curve of Jake's arm, already retreating from the fray.

7

BY THE TIME the weekend was over and Siobhan was back in her apartment with a glowing Maura, she was sure that her headache was permanent and that she wouldn't be able to unclench her teeth without surgery.

Plunging right back into rehearsals for the television show allowed her to give full vent to her growing aggression.

"Dammit Siobhan, that hurt. Aren't you enough of an actress to pull your punches?" Gareth Lane, the second leading man on the show, laid the palm of his hand on his jaw. "You really pack a wallop. I'll need makeup to cover the bruise tomorrow, you can bet on that." He walked away from her while she was still apologizing to him.

Del Krantz came up to her, Hughy at his heels. "If you're trying to cut down the work force on 'Day by Day' you're doing one hell of a job, Siobhan." Del squinted at her. "But you did one hell of a job of acting today—which probably hurt Gareth more than your left jab."

"You were sensational, Siobhan—stellar stuff," Hughy chortled. "I don't think Gareth thought anyone could upstage him, but you did today."

She gasped. "I didn't mean to do that. I guess I forgot myself, got into the part a little too much."

Del flapped his hand. "Don't knock a good perfor-

mance. I should get such feeling from the rest of them."
He walked toward a cluster of actors and script assistants, a scowl on his face.

"Del is right, sweetie. It was a great piece of work. It will set fire to the TV screens."

Siobhan felt her face give way. "Now you make me feel like Joan of Arc."

"What is it with you? I know you're upset about something but you won't talk to me. Haven't we always talked over our problems with each other?"

"Yes, but you already know my problem, and neither you nor I can solve it, short of murder." Siobhan sighed, then patted Hughy on the arm to show she was sorry for lashing out at him.

"I think he loves you." Hughy looked like a basset hound for a moment.

"Maybe. Or maybe he just thinks he does—or maybe he will for a short time. Any of which is a no-win situation for me." She choked out a laugh.

"His parents will be in the audience this evening when we tape the show, and so will mine. Then there's a party at the Wilsons'." Hughy grimaced. "Frances Wilson is a very dear person but her husband is a consummate bore and a snob. But it's all planned, so . . . ."

"Hughy, I am not going to do anything that will endanger your relationship with Maura, or make either of you a laughingstock. Which is why I would rather not go . . . but I'm going."

"I wish this was what you wanted, Siobhan." Hughy looked more hangdog than ever.

"I am very happy that you and Maura are together. Your lives together promise to be very full and good."

"You sound like a first-grader reading from a primer." Hughy shook his head. "It would be so easy if you were a bit of fluff, the type that Jake used to drag around with him."

"Don't give me chapter and verse of his love life, please," she interjected quickly.

"I wasn't going to do that. Get changed and we'll pick up Maura and have dinner at my apartment." He paused. "That is, unless Jake is taking you out to dinner."

The evening before, Siobhan remembered, he had told her he would see her that night. She had the feeling he had meant dinner. But, since he hadn't spelled it out. . . . "Lovely. Why don't we stop at the Lotus Room and get takeout for three."

"Genius." Hughy closed his eyes. "I love Chinese food."

"I know."

Fifteen minutes later they had picked up Maura and were on their way to the apartment.

"Shouldn't I change before we eat? Wash up or something?" Maura wailed as they reentered the car after stopping at the Lotus Room for their food.

"Change later, my love. Better to eat this while it's hot." Hughy grinned at his lady.

"I really feel I should drive when I'm with the two of you." Siobhan said from her seat near the passenger door. "All you ever do is make sheep's eyes at each other."

"Sheep! Don't mention them. It reminds me of being out in the fields on the station and trying to herd the stupid things," Maura said disgustedly, poking Hughy in the arm when he laughed.

"I'd love to see the station," Hughy told her.

"Me, too," Siobhan nodded, missing her mother with a sudden, nagging ache.

"It is beautiful," Maura admitted. "But I could never get the hang of things like the rest of the Butler gang. You should see Simon and Ross work the sheep, sis. You'd be shocked. They're true Aussies."

"Perhaps I will go to see mother one day." She swallowed, the sting of tears in her throat as she got out of the car and waited for Maura before shutting the door.

"I thought I would join the party—unless it's private." Jake pushed away from the wall near the elevator and walked toward them, his softly enunciated words telegraphing his anger.

"Jake, how wonderful," Maura called, then threw herself at him and kissed him. "Join us. We have Chinese."

"I would like to see your big sister be as welcoming as you are, little sister." Jake kissed Maura's nose, then looked over her head at Siobhan. "Didn't I tell you that I would see you this evening?"

"Yes, but I assumed that it would be after the show."

"Did you?" he drawled, nodding to Hughy, as he joined the others in the elevator.

The ascent to Hughy's floor was made in silence, Maura shooting puzzled looks at her fiancé, who shushed her.

When Hughy opened his door, Siobhan went to the kitchen at once to put on the kettle for the herbal tea they would be drinking with their food.

"Siobhan, I don't like it when you lie to me. And don't bother to tell me that you didn't know I'd be picking you up. You know damn well that I'd want you to eat something before you went in front of the cameras." Jake had followed her into the kitchen.

She swallowed and said nothing, filling the kettle, then putting it on the stove. She wanted to kill him and apologize all at the same time. She jumped when she felt his hands on her shoulders, his mouth at the base of her neck, caressing her skin.

"Let's call a truce. I don't want you upset before your performance. You might smack someone on the set."

She turned in his embrace, bringing her arms up around his waist. "Oh Jake, I already did that today. I smacked Gareth so hard I . . . I think he might sue me." She gave a shaky laugh.

"Let him try," Jake chuckled, his eyes softening. "I hated it when I couldn't find you at the studio—"

"Hey, you two, bring some forks from the drawer and hurry. This food is going to get cold," Hughy called from the other room.

Jake leaned his forehead against hers. "Interruptions, all the time." He looked at her. "Do you suppose we could be alone sometime?"

"I'd like that, but Lance is staying at your place . . ." Siobhan shrugged.

"Eighteen more days and you'll be Mrs. Deerfield," Jake muttered, turning to look at the now-whistling kettle.

"Are you sure you want to be shackled by marriage?"

His head whipped back, his stare pinning her like a butterfly to a board. "Get any ideas you may have of changing your mind about this marriage out of your head, love. It's on and it stays on. And tonight, after the party at the Wilsons', we are going to have a talk."

Siobhan fumbled in the drawer next to her and dragged out the cutlery. "Forks." She waved them in front of Jake's face. "Time to eat."

"You are forever trying to put me off, my darling," Jake took hold of her wrist and pulled her against his chest. "But you mustn't forget that there is only so much

I will let you get away with." He kissed her as she started to open her mouth, his tongue intruding and teasing hers, his lips like silken steel against hers.

He nipped her soft underlip with his white teeth, released her, turned and left the room all in one fluid motion.

"Tyrant," she gasped, gulping deep breaths to steady herself.

"Siobhan, when you come, Hughy said to bring the white wine chilling in the refrigerator," Maura caroled, happiness in every syllable.

"Coming." Her shaking hand seized the bottle and closed the fridge door. Then she managed to get a clean towel from the rack to wrap around the dewy, cold glass.

When she went back into the lounge, the other three were sitting on cushions on the floor, looking at her.

"Hurry, we're starved and we don't have too long for dinner," implored Hughy.

As was her custom, Siobhan didn't eat much, but she was able to have two glasses of the chilled Chablis.

"Take it easy, darling." Jake leaned toward her.

"Oh, I'm fine." She smiled at him without really seeing him. Her mind was in chaos. She knew from experience that this came partly from doing the show. It was as though her whole system went on hold before camera time—and with Jake at her side, she seemed to have gone totally numb.

It seemed only minutes later that she was sitting beside Jake in his car, heading back to the studio.

He took hold of her knee and squeezed gently. "Are you nervous, love?"

"I'm always a little off the mark before we shoot." She put her hand down to push his fingers away, but instead found herself clutching at his hand as if it were a lifeline.

Conversation was desultory for the rest of the ride, but some of her gray feelings began to change to beige, then to orange and finally to pink. Of course she could handle the show. Her confidence returned in such a surge that she gasped with the power of it.

"What is it, love?" Jake quizzed her as he stepped from the car. He handed his keys to an attendant, then came around the vehicle to help her alight.

"Nothing, I feel better." She smiled up at him.

They hurried into the building, where she left him to go to her dressing room and change into the seductive outfit she would wear for the show that evening. Sometimes she had as many as five changes, but tonight there would be just one.

Siobhan slipped on the one-piece, peach-colored party pajama outfit, the top strapless and low on her full breasts. She gulped when she looked at herself. "There isn't a great deal of me left to the imagination," she muttered, tossing a makeup cape around her shoulders to put the finishing touches to her face.

When she left her room, she heard the low, appreciative whistle from Willy, the assistant stage-manager. She made a face at him and laughed.

Jake appeared in front of her as she made her way to the studio. He looked her over from head to foot, his eyes finishing on her mouth. "I could eat you with a very small spoon."

"I don't think that's in my job description." Siobhan breathed, reeling from the impact of Jake's presence.

He stayed with her until it was time for the performers to take their places. Then he folded her in his arms. "Kiss me, darling."

Without conscious thought, she obeyed, her eyes

closing and her arms lifting up around his neck, her tongue sparring with his.

"Don't, love..." Jake was out of breath, his laugh shaky. He drew one finger down her nose. "You are so beautiful in those peach pajamas..." he frowned for a moment as he looked down on her "...but shouldn't you wear a jacket or something...all your lovely skin showing...the tops of your breasts, the way that silk wraps so tightly around your legs...."

"Jake," she gave a breathless laugh, wanting him never to stop looking at her. "This outfit has no jacket. The strapless top is supposed to be cut low and the bottoms are wraparound silk, like the bottoms of harem pants."

"But with harem pants you'd wear a tunic—and those damned orange high heels...." Jake tightened his hold on her.

"Siobhan, get a move on." Del had come looking for her, his irritation evident.

"I kept her." Jake gave the other man a level look.

"Coming." Siobhan kissed Jake once quickly on the mouth, then followed Del, her rapid pulse having nothing to do with the show.

In moments, she became Raine, infusing the role with the electric sensitivity that Jake had aroused in her.

"Don't touch me, you creep," Raine raged at Sam, played by Gareth. Their fight scene took on the power emanating from Jake to Siobhan. It fairly exploded with feeling.

When Gareth struck her as the scene called for, Siobhan knew at once that he had put more in the punch than there should have been, but she was so high on her own feelings that she didn't lose a jot of her timing. When the moment came for her to lash back at him, she put a spin on the blow she sent him, taking satisfaction when he reeled back.

"You did that on purpose," he hissed to her when the cameras focused on the actors coming into the scene.

"You hit me too hard and you know it! You had that coming," Siobhan hissed back.

The rest of the cast seemed to catch the feeling and the show finished on a very high note, the studio audience and the crew applauding with gusto at the end.

Backstage, Siobhan rubbed at her face and turned when she heard her name.

"You ever try that on me again, Siobhan . . ." Gareth glared.

"Now, look, you . . ." she began. Her eyes widened as she looked past Gareth at Jake, coming down the hall like a bull on the charge, his father hanging on one arm, Hughy on the other. Neither man seemed to be slowing him down appreciably.

"Siobhan," Hughy yelled, jerking his head at Jake.

"Gareth, if you value your job and your life, you had better leave. Now!" Siobhan pushed at the actor, urging him to move.

"What the hell?" An angry Gareth looked over his shoulder. "Christ, what's got into him?"

"He's mine and he's mad," Siobhan informed him beatifically as Jake advanced toward them.

"I damn well didn't know you had a standing army," Gareth wheezed, his head wheeling as he looked for an escape.

"Go down the hall the other way, then through the women's dressing room. Unlike you, Jake's too much of a gentleman to look there first. By the time he does, you can be out the side door. Hurry," she urged, trying to gauge the speed of Jake's charge.

"Damn you, Siobhan," Gareth cursed, then took to his heels.

Jake charged past, still towing his father and Hughy.

"Hello darling," Siobhan cooed. "Aren't you going to kiss me?"

Jake's father looked at her gratefully.

Jake stopped dead and looked at her. "Are you protecting that scum from the beating he deserves?" He tried to pull Hughy from one arm.

She shook her head. "I'm protecting you from a jail sentence." Siobhan reached up and kissed him on the mouth, feeling his immediate response.

"Let go, Hughy, I'm not going anywhere. But that creep better stay out of my way. He didn't pull his punch when he socked you." Jake stepped closer to her and lifted her chin with one finger, his lips tightening as he looked at her left cheek. "You'll have a bruise there in the morning."

"So will he."

A reluctant grin stretched Jake's mouth. "I saw that, too. You have quite a left, lady mine. I didn't even know you were left-handed."

"I'm not." She ignored Del who had come up to see if she had any damage to her face. "But when I was little, my father taught me to jab. I rather liked it."

Jake laughed, the last of the fury lines leaving his face. "I'll have to be careful. I could lose some teeth."

"Scared, huh?" Siobhan leaned against him as they strolled away from the others.

"Terrified," Jake grinned at her. Then his grin faded for a moment. "But I'll be watching that creep and if he makes one wrong move...."

"He won't." She patted his cheek. "I have to change and get ready."

"Can I come and help you?" Jake groaned against her ear.

"Don't be silly. I'll be right with you."

As she walked away from him, he called to her again, making her turn around to face him.

"Do you mind not wearing that outfit you have on? I'm getting damn sick of cold showers."

"Poor baby." Laughter trilled out of her, getting an answering glitter from him.

"Hurry."

She nodded and sped away, her feet only touching ground at every other step.

As she dressed in the lavender satin two-piece suit, the skirt short, the jacket boxy with a frilly silk blouse in palest violet to wear under it, she studied her reflection in the long mirror next to the dressing table. "You're a fool to play the game, Siobhan Ryan Butler. You're the one whose heart will be packed in cement and dropped into the river. Jake will go on to live a full life and yours will be in pieces."

She listened as she talked out loud to herself and nodded. "Yes, I will be hurt and smashed, but I'll have memories. I think I would rather have something. If I have to protect myself against hurt, I'll have nothing. I'm taking the chance," she decided at that moment, her face in the mirror reflecting the shock she was feeling at finally deciding on a course of action.

She slipped the black-silk slings on her feet, picked up the matching clutch bag and strolled from the room. She would lose Jake, then she would run and hide. In the meantime, she was going to try out some of the joys of life.

She walked up to where Jake was standing with his and Hughy's parents. Hughy and Maura were at one side, smiling into each other's eyes. "I hope they have music at this party. I feel like dancing," Siobhan said before she hugged Jess Deerfield and kissed David's cheek, shook hands with the Prentices and smiled at Hughy and Maura.

"Am I being ignored?" Jake stepped in front of her.

"Of course not, darling." She stood on tiptoe and kissed his mouth, the palm of her hand resting on that fresh-shaved face. "How was that?"

"Not bad." Jake took her arm, leading her toward the elevators and telling the others to hurry.

"Is Lance not invited?" She was content to be crowded against Jake in the elevator.

"He was invited to the Temples' for dinner. Remember their pretty daughter? The brunette with all the curls?"

Siobhan smiled and nodded, letting him lead her from the elevator, content when he told the others that he was taking her in his car and that they would meet at the Wilsons'.

"What happened?"

Siobhan jumped at the rapid-fire words from Jake's mouth. "What are you talking about?"

"Sweetie, don't play games with me. You change your mood more often than a chameleon changes colors, but playing the devoted fiancée is a new one." His strong hands roved the wheel of the car, clenching and unclenching, the movement of his jaw the same rhythm. "What's the new game all about, Siobhan?"

She swallowed. "I thought you wanted me to be a loving bride-to-be."

"I thought so too, but the only emotion I'm feeling at the moment is suspicion."

"What a shame! The great James Kendall Deerfield

worried about a woman after having the female popula-
tion of Cleveland hovering about him," she snapped.

"Not quite, angel." Jake shot back.

"How is it in all that time, with all those women, you
never managed to get married?"

"I came close once—but a week before the ceremony
she hopped a flight for Tangier and married an Arab
sheik."

She felt vengeful and elated at the same time. "How
awful for you. You must have been pretty down."

"I was for about three days, then I decided that I was
a lucky man. I had never loved Denise but her family
and mine were good friends . . ." he shrugged. "You may
see her this evening at the Wilsons'."

Siobhan blinked and turned to face him. "Will that
bother you?"

"Hell, no. I've seen Dee many times since her divorce."

"I see."

"No, you don't see. I've seen her in the company of
her parents and other friends."

"Oh."

Jake laughed, a low silken growl that crawled up her
spine like a butterfly. "You delight me, angel."

"Oh."

The Wilson home was a discreetly elegant brownstone with an old-fashioned wrought-iron street lamp
out front and twin grillwork gates that stood open in
greeting.

"What a friendly house," Siobhan murmured. "It in-
vites you in with a smile from those leaded-glass windows."

"Shall we house-hunt for one like it? We can sell the
apartment and look for a brownstone, if you like."

Siobhan blinked at the casual tone. She almost said that she thought it would take a long time to pay for it, when she remembered that Jake had probably never saved for anything in his life.

"You're changing color to fade—out black. What is it this time?" he whispered, just as the door was opened by a man in a black suit. "Ah, good evening Loomis. How are you?"

"Fine, Mr. Jake. The mister and missus are expecting you. You'll find them in the lounge, sir," said the man with the tufted white hair and brown eyes, who nodded and smiled at Siobhan.

"This is my fiancée, Loomis. Miss Siobhan Ryan Butler."

She put out her hand, knowing that it wasn't de rigueur to shake hands with the help, but she found Loomis very appealing.

Loomis looked at her hand, then took it with great care and shook it once before ushering them to the door of a larger room.

"He's your slave for life. I wish you would stop doing that. I will be having to fight men off with cannons."

Siobhan looked up at him, feeling a heat rise in her at the look in his eyes. "He's a nice man."

"That he is."

Mrs. Wilson came forward in a rush, embracing both Siobhan and Jake. "My dear, your performance was masterful tonight." Her birdlike eyes fixed on Siobhan's cheek. "I see you do have a mark on your face after that wrestling match with the actor. Should you be so realistic, my dear?"

"Siobhan won't be doing such 'realistic' scenes again." Jake assured the thin woman he called Aunt Sarah.

"Good." She took Jake and Siobhan by the arm and

led them into the lounge. "I'm sure you know everyone here, Jake, but you must introduce Siobhan."

She was whirled around the room, trying to field the many questions about her television show and her upcoming marriage to Jake. She felt she handled herself well enough at first.

"And darling, this is Denise Teller." Jake's mouth quirked in a smile as he watched Siobhan, who stared first at him, then turned slowly to greet the tiny, very chic brunette, her hair like a black velvet cap, her large eyes a tobacco brown, her figure curvy and sexy. The cherry-red silk was swathed around her body sarong-style.

"How do you do, Miss Teller," Siobhan smiled, wishing for a moment that she was a shark so she might tear that look from Denise Teller's face.

"Do call me Denise." She turned to Jake and draped herself over him. "Darling, she's so tall. And you always told me you liked petite women."

"Did I?" Jake grinned at her, then looked at Siobhan. "It must have been a lie."

"Tell her to talk to your mother," Denise pouted.

"If you don't take your hands off my Jake, I'm going to tip you upside down and shake you by the heels," Siobhan leaned forward and cooed to Denise.

Jake laughed. "Naughty girl." He kissed her cheek, not even turning around when Denise flounced away. "I don't think you could have lifted her. Denise is heavier than you. I think."

"She couldn't be. She's petite," Siobhan glowered at him when he chuckled and pulled her closer.

"She does not appeal to me." Jake looked down into her eyes.

"You're just saying that because you don't want me to

give you my left jab." The surge of relief she felt threatened to swamp her.

"Right," he chortled, bending his head and nipping at her chin. "Did I tell you that I love the taste of your skin? That I'm going to spend the first few weeks we're married just sipping you?"

"Cannibal," she squeaked, feeling her knees give way.

Jake looked around the room, his arm still gripping her waist. "I think you've met everyone, so why don't we dance a little before someone comes to try and separate us?"

"Please," she breathed, delighted by the nape of his neck as her fingers feathered upward into his hair. "I like your curls."

"Love..." Jake bent over her as they swayed to a slow ballad, "...if you continue to do that, we may be leaving earlier than expected."

"Shame on you, Mr. Deerfield." She and Jake moved closer to the musicians just as the music stopped.

"Hi, doll, how are you? Remember me? George Madison from New Paltz." The balding man at the piano stood and put out his hand to Siobhan.

She felt Jake stiffen at her side as she moved closer and took the outstretched hand, finally placing George's face. "Of course, now I remember. No mayo on the sandwich but heavy on the ketchup." She laughed.

"How original! David, you're getting a daughter-in-law who can always moonlight as a waitress if the money doesn't hold out."

Siobhan whirled to find Denise standing next to Jake's father and some of the other guests looking at her curiously.

"If my wife-to-be would like to be a waitress instead of the successful actress she is, then I would have no problem with that..." Jake grated, his fingers digging into her waist.

Denise opened her brown eyes to their widest.

David Deerfield looked at his son, then at Siobhan. "Siobhan, my dear, I think this is our dance." He took her hand in his and led her out onto a section of parquet floor reserved for dancing.

For long moments they circled the floor in silence. Finally David spoke. "Did I ever tell you how my father got his start in the shipping business, my child?"

"Ah, no...I don't think so." Siobhan let her eyes slip over him for a moment.

"He had a small cart down on the wharf in Manhattan where he would buy fish from the boats that came in. Then he would push the cart downtown and sell the fish to restaurants. He was eventually able to buy a fishing boat of his own. By the time I was about ten or eleven I would push the cart down to the restaurants after school. Then he bought another boat and he and my mother moved out of the tenement apartment into our first house. I won't bore you with all the details, but my father had a fleet of fishing boats and tankers before he died, plus several of the restaurants that he had sold fish to when he began his business. After his death, when I took over I began to branch out even more—into trucking and frozen foods. Now Jake has a good percentage of my business, but he also has a going concern of his own in—"

"Computers." Siobhan smiled up at the man who would be her father-in-law in a little over two weeks.

"Right. But I have never forgotten the fish that I used to push to the downtown eateries—"

"So if I want a job as a waitress, I had better do it at one of the family-owned places." Her laughter spilled out of her, almost smothered by the booming laugh of her dancing partner.

"Right. You're a good girl, Siobhan. My wife can't wait for you to become our daughter. And now that I'm beginning to know you better, I guess I can't wait, either."

"Thank you, sir," she gulped.

"I'm glad you're not going to cry. I wouldn't want Jake to come over here and punch me in the nose."

"He wouldn't do that," she giggled.

"My dear, before today, I would have agreed with you, even though I have always known that my son was one tough cookie who had to fight to keep his temper in check. After I saw the reaction when you and that actor were fighting, I knew he wouldn't stand for anyone coming near you—not even his father—so you keep smiling."

"Yes, sir." Siobhan sighed with relief.

Jake tapped his father on the shoulder. "Father, I think you've had her long enough."

"I was just telling her one of my stories." His father glared at Jake.

"No way. Those tales take forever." Jake insisted, reaching around his father to ease Siobhan free of him.

"And she was listening too." His father scowled at him. Then he kissed his future daughter-in-law on the cheek. "We'll have lunch one day and I'll tell you all my stories."

"I'd like that," she chuckled.

"Lord, will you be sorry." Jake said against her temple. "Would you like to leave now?"

She looked up at him and nodded. "I just want to speak to your mother and say good-night to the Prentices."

"Fine," Jake inhaled. "You look lovely tonight."

"Thank you."

They strolled hand in hand around the room, saying good-night to their hosts and to some of the guests.

When they stopped in front of Jessamyn Deerfield, Jake's mother smiled at Siobhan as Jake stepped to one side to speak to a friend. "I haven't given up on our campaign to rout the Deerfield men but . . ." she looked rueful, ". . . it may have to wait ten years or so until we can catch them off guard."

"At *least!*" Siobhan laughed, liking the spirited, diminutive lady who was to be her mother-in-law.

"We'll lie low until they're lulled into a false sense of security," Jess whispered.

"It might be twenty years," Siobhan whispered back.

"That's all right, dear. We'll be patient."

"And wear a suit of armor."

"Shhh, dear, here comes Jake." His mother gave him a big smile as he walked up to them.

"Good night mother. Please stop including my intended in your schemes." Jake kissed her cheek.

"Good night, dear boy. I don't know what you're talking about."

Jake led Siobhan from the house, chuckling to himself. "Not to worry, darling. I am not going to ask you what my mother is trying to embroil you in—now."

Siobhan opened her mouth and shut it again, glaring at Jake when he laughed.

"I've known her too long, love."

"Omniscient, are you?" she bit off the words.

"Where you and my mother are concerned, maybe a tad," he chuckled.

Siobhan could feel her nostrils flaring as she fumed inwardly. Know-it-all!

"Call me the names out loud, sweetheart," Jake directed in soft ones.

"Pompous ass," she hissed. Then she became aware that they had driven down into an underground garage. She knew that it was too short a drive to be her building. "Where are we?"

Jake parked and looked at her, his arm on the steering wheel. "I want you to come up and see my flat. If you don't like it, we can redecorate. Or we can find something else."

Siobhan watched him for a moment, then she nodded.

When Jake came around the car and handed her out, she could feel the tremor go up her body in reaction to his nearness. "I know a couple of good decorators..." Jake began.

"Perhaps we could do it ourselves," she ventured as they rode the private elevator upward.

Jake grimaced as he nodded to her to precede him into a foyer. "That sounds too involved and time-consuming."

"Actually, I find changing things over much to my taste," Siobhan said.

"Oh, sure. Do some things if you want to, but for the main theme, we'll call a professional...."

"I see." She turned away.

Jake put his arm around her and led her down into the stark, modern front room, all color abstracted from the scheme of black and white. "Too strong for you?" Jake laughed.

"Too stark."

"Tell me your favorite color—besides your favorite blue."

"Blue, blue, shades of blue, hues of blue."

Jake shrugged. "We'll start with that and let the professionals do their best."

"Or worst."

"It's a good thing you danced so much this evening..." He gave her a hard grin. "...or you would be more than just outspoken. You would probably be reeling."

Siobhan could feel her chin jut forward. "If my plain speaking about this abomination you call 'professional decorating' offends you, don't hide your feelings. Speak up."

Jake looked at her, arms akimbo, head to one side. "Wanna wrestle?"

Siobhan inhaled, then moved toward him, hands clenched and up, teeth locked together.

Jake met her halfway, ducking his head when she swung at him and tossing her over his shoulder. Striding down some steps he headed toward the fireplace and the mammoth horseshoe couch beside it.

"Put me down." Siobhan pummeled his back from her upside-down position. "That was foul play." Anger and laughter warred in her.

Jake flipped her up again, but before she could regain her equilibrium, he pulled her down on top of him as he sat on the couch. "Now what were you saying about being fair?" His mouth roved up one cheek and down the other. "Mmm, you taste so good."

"You're repeating yourself," she gulped, bringing her hand up to hit him and then deciding to caress and rub his cheek instead. "Your beard has a stubble already."

"Then I shall shave it." Jake heaved himself upward, his hard muscles pushing him to his feet. "Better yet, you can shave me."

"You wouldn't let a woman shave you."

"Try me." Jake let her slide down his body, then put out his hand to her.

When she put her hand in his, he clasped her close to him at once, leading her out of the room and across a hall. "Jake, this might not be a good idea."

"To shave me? Darling, I trust you not to cut me."

"You know that isn't what I was talking about." She took a deep breath when he opened the middle door in the upper hall.

The bedroom was stark like the rest of the apartment. But there was a subtle difference. Perhaps it was the cream and beige color scheme or the touches of oak wood and the overstuffed chairs opposite the fireplace. Siobhan only knew that she preferred it to the front room.

"I like this better than the lounge, so I guess I was wrong about the decorator," she offered, looking up at him as he stood at her side.

"Not so wrong. I insisted on the color scheme and the desk and chairs." He turned her toward the bed. "And I ordered the extra-sized bed, too."

"Good thinking."

"Do you like the bed?"

"Didn't you want me to shave you?"

"Please."

The bathroom echoed the color scheme of the bedroom, the tiles having a Spanish peasant scene painted on them.

"The azuelos are beautiful," she whispered as she watched Jake lather his chin, then turn and hand her a double-edged razor. "I assumed that you used an electric shaver." She turned white, taking the razor in a loose grasp.

"No, darling, I use an electric at the office, but I use this at home."

"I don't think I can do it." Siobhan wavered as Jake
sat on the vanity counter and leaned toward her. She
began lathering more shaving cream into her hand, then
smoothing it on his face.

"Go ahead, my lovely. Being cut by you would be
like being kissed by anyone else."

"You poet," she shivered. Taking more deep breaths,
she let the razor come down his face and neck in
smooth, even strokes, gaining confidence as she pro-
gressed. It took considerable time, but she finished and
Jake's face was uncut and as smooth as if he had done it
himself.

"Mmm, I loved that. After we're married, you can
shave me every morning. Except when you're angry
with me."

She watched his face come toward her, opening her
mouth to tell him that it was time for her to go home.
Instead, the moment she felt his tongue pressing her
own, her eyes closed and her arms came up around his
neck.

8

As was her usual custom, Siobhan woke before dawn, rose and went to the bathroom. Ever since she had worked in the diner, she had arisen before the sun and staggered to the bathroom. It had only been a short time ago that she had been able to stop herself from showering at that ungodly hour. Now, as she washed her hands and groaned at her sleep-frazzled image, she swore to herself to break the before-dawn rising habit.

"Here you are," Jake yawned as he pushed open the door.

"Aaagh," Siobhan crossed her hands in front of her as she faced him in the mirror. "What are you doing here?"

Jake leaned against the doorjamb and yawned again. "I live here. Now that you have me up, may I use the bathroom?"

"Yes," she retreated trying to squeeze by him.

"Go back to bed." He leaned forward, his stubble an erotic abrasion on her skin. "I can read your mind, darling, so don't try to dress and get out of the apartment." He rubbed her derriere as he released her. "Mmm, so nice."

She galloped to the bed, for the first time taking note of her surroundings. "You're a damn fool, Siobhan Butler," she scourged herself. "How could you get out of bed and go to the bathroom and not realize you weren't in your own apartment." She muttered this with the silk sheets clutched over her head. "Don't you know enough to get up and go home?"

"Are we playing games?" Jake whispered, lifting the sheet and looking down at her. "I like games."

"I'll buy you a jump rope." She scrambled for her edge of the sheet as he settled into the bed and slid toward her. "Silk sheets are very slippery aren't they?"

His long, muscular arm curled around her middle and drew her to him. "Don't try to get away from me, love. You know it won't work. I have no intention of looking for you again."

"You didn't look for me," she stared at him, immobilized when she saw the blood climbing up his face. Jake Deerfield blushing! Did elephants fly?

"I looked for you." His mouth dropped to her breast, the gentle tug of his lips on her nipple like rockets exploding in her bloodstream. "And now you're here with me." His mouth came up her neck as though he had to explore every pore, follow every vein and artery. "Did I tell you that I'm crazy about your outfit?"

"I'm...I'm not wearing anything." Siobhan felt the words fall off her lips as she reached out one finger to pull the curling hair on his chest. She felt goose bumps all over her body when he moaned, "I know."

"Having a good time, love?" His throaty chuckle stirred her blood.

"It beats waiting on tables," she gulped as Jake stroked the faint down on her thighs.

"It beats anything on the planet," Jake muttered, his head sliding down her body as his tongue massaged, soothing and exciting her all in one lovely sweep down, then up again. "You're like a sugared strawberry, angel mine."

"Jake..." she had trouble saying more as her hands

began to touch him, find him, want him, smooth over him like an invisible oil. As her hands slid down his muscular chest with its sensual quilting, she came in contact with the manhood of him, her hand pausing, fluttering there, yearning yet hesitant.

"Darling, please feel me—since you are my lady, and you make me this way." His slumberous eyes fixed on her as he slid up her body.

Her hands clenched on his waist, then her fingers flexed on that tough, erotic flesh. Floating over him once more, her hands brought his writhing body in contact with hers. His heart seemed to accelerate at the contact and all her reasons for leaving Jake seemed to explode into tiny fragments.

Their mouths came together like homing devices as they interlocked fingers and breathed into each other. It stunned Siobhan that she was both unbearably excited and comfortable, that she could have stayed with her mouth locked on Jake's until time ended.

"Baby, it's always so new, but it feels the same way it did the first time with you. Tell me you want me, that you feel it, too." Jake mumbled against her body as they moved together in building rhythm.

"I'll give you an affidavit . . ." her words tumbled out of her mouth as she held him to her, her body twisting away in a cocoon of love. "Jake!" she called out, her body aching and straining to take him and hold him enmeshed in her for all time.

"All yesterday while I was giving dictation, I thought of you. My secretary asked me—oh, Siobhan, don't stop—do it—"

"What did your secretary say?" she had trouble with the question, her breathing so erratic she wasn't in control of her words.

"She asked me if I really wanted to open my letter to the Kelso Corporation with 'My darling Siobhan.'"

She giggled in delight. "Liar."

"No...true...I thought...Siobhan...you're pulling me apart...." Jake rolled her under him and entered her with gentle persistence as her body bucked in response. "You'll have to edit all my letters," Jake told her, his smile quivering over her.

She laughed out loud, feeling free, yet fettered with love, knowing that she could fly, but content to be captured by Jake.

"Darling, when you laugh—"

Siobhan reared, hearing him call out in harsh passion as her body thrust back at his, then she was beyond hearing and seeing as the world spun in front of her, small planets and stars exploding behind her eyes as they passed every meteor on their journey into golden light.

Siobhan opened her eyes some time later and knew that she had slept. Her body jerked upward and she blinked at Jake.

"We have to shower, darling. I'm late as it is—but it was worth it." He kissed her full on the mouth, pulling her to her feet in one motion then leading her into the bathroom, clamped to his side. His arm reached in lazy fashion for the soap and shampoo, as he turned on the shower with his other hand. "I'll do you, and you do me, lady mine."

"We'll never leave the bathroom and I really do— what is it? What's wrong? Why are you glaring at me?"

"That damn bruise." Jake touched her cheek, pulling her free of the cascading water so that he could study her skin.

"Jake, it's over. Don't make trouble about it now, please...."

A muscle twitched at the side of his mouth, then he was holding her close to him as they stood again under the spray. "No one is going to hit you—not ever."

She cuddled close to him and began to wash his hair, then his body.

"Mmm, good, don't stop. The ultimate massage. . . ."

"Sybarite." She ran her fingers through his hair, rinsing it.

When they finally finished in the shower and went down to Jake's kitchen to have juice, coffee and toast, they were both late.

"I don't give a damn what Del says to you. You don't have any more key scenes in this segment. Having you in the hospital all bandaged up from the beating writes you out of the script for the month we'll be away." Jake was grim-faced as he spread jam on her toast and set it in front of her. "And take those vitamin pills, too."

"Yes, sir. I know I'm out of the shooting for now, but there still might be things Del would want for publicity. He did want me down there at nine."

Jake looked at her in brooding concentration. "I don't like you working. I don't like other men around you." He held up his hand when she opened her mouth to speak. "I know, I know, I'll have to live with it."

"You are a nutty man." She put her index finger on his nose.

He bent his head back and caught the digit in his mouth, sucking it. "All of you tastes good, darling." He chuckled. "I love it when your face gets red."

Siobhan poked her tongue at him as she lifted the dishes, then took them to the sink and rinsed them.

"Leave them for the—"

"Don't you dare say it. I know how much extra work

dirty, encrusted dishes can be, so don't say that I shouldn't scrape them and rinse them."

Jake shrugged and left the room, whistling.

She sighed, put the dishes in the drainer to be stacked in the dishwasher by the housekeeper, and then followed him up the stairs.

He met her at the top with a toothbrush. "I thought you might need this."

Déjà vu! Siobhan recalled the moment she had taken the toothbrush from him, years ago when she had just met him. Her smile wavered as she looked at him.

Puzzled, Jake took her arm as they walked toward the bathroom. "You looked like someone walked on your grave."

She smiled at him again and told him she would be right with him.

In the car, driving through the Manhattan traffic, Jake's hand rested on her knee. "I knew you couldn't hold out any more than I could."

"What do you mean?" Siobhan pushed down her sun visor and looked into the mirror to see if Jake had smeared her lipstick when he had kissed her as they entered the car.

"That stuff about holding off until we were married. That was crazy. Both of us wanted and needed to be together."

"A little abstinence is not a sin."

"That's archaic, love. Men and women don't wait when they want something. They take it and enjoy it."

"Then they sometimes discard it just as fast because they sacrificed nothing to get it when it's all so easy."

Jake shrugged, watching the traffic. "Some get rid of their partners, some don't. Still, it makes no sense to deny ourselves when we both want each other."

Siobhan looked at that tough, rock-hewn profile as though it had just been struck in bronze. She didn't know this man! This was Jake Deerfield, the entrepreneur, the industrialist, the builder, one tough man to cross, as Hughy had called him. He was no different now than when he had first taken her to his home, made love to her and assumed she would be around for him whenever he chose to summon her. She bit her lip. And she was no different from the waitress who had gone with him and had given him her body, and her love.

"Well, love, are you going to stop daydreaming and go to work?"

Her head jerked up and she looked around her at the door leading to the station entrance for employees. Then she looked again at Jake. "I didn't thank you for all the clothes you bought for me." She looked down at the pale violet and blue tweed suit in wrinkle-free cotton that she was wearing. "I'm amazed your secretary was able to get so many things in the. . . ."

"Wrong." Jake leaned over and kissed her nose. "I am a very busy man and I delegate a great deal of my work. But the really important things like picking out my lady's clothes, I do myself—with a little help from top designers." He smiled at her in an assessing way, seemingly unaware that they were parked in a No Parking zone. "What's bothering you, love?"

"Nothing. Thank you again for the clothes. . . ."

"See you tonight." Before she could open the door, Jake turned her toward him, his mouth closing over hers. "I need my kiss."

"Ah. . . Jake, don't pick me up tonight. I'm so tired—"

"Wonder why . . ." he mumbled against her neck.

"—that I think I'll just have a light supper and get to bed."

Jake studied her for long moments, then nodded. "All right. But I won't like not seeing you tonight."

She kissed him again, letting her tongue run along his lips and into his mouth.

"Siobhan, let's go home."

"Goodbye, Jake," she breathed, getting out of the car, feeling his eyes on her as she crossed the sidewalk to the building. As she opened the door, she heard the car pull away.

She went right to Del's office, knocked once and entered, knowing that the director had already been at his desk for at least half an hour before the rest of the force was due to stagger in.

"What's this, my dear Siobhan, looking harried after the fabulous reviews you've had this morning?" A gleeful Del pushed a newspaper across the desk at her.

She hardly glanced at it. "Del, listen. I have leave coming and you can shoot around me. I have to go away. I'll be in touch—"

Del surged to his feet, as though he would argue with her. Then he looked at the way she was wringing her hands. "All right, love. No questions asked—but only for you."

"Don't tell anyone we had this talk. I just want to get away."

He nodded. "Shall I get someone to accompany you home?"

She shook her head and left, catching a cab to the apartment she shared with Maura. Maura! Siobhan felt guilty that she hadn't gone out the front way past the reception desk and explained to her sister that she was leaving.

"No, no, I can't explain even to you, Maura . . ." she mumbled to herself in the back of the cab, paying the

man too much when she stepped out in front of her
building.

Once in the apartment, she sent a wire to her mother,
checked to see if the passport she had used to do publicity in England was still valid, then sat down and wrote a
long letter to Maura and Lance. She wrote a much
shorter one to Jake, enclosing in his envelope the emerald she had worn on her left hand.

Siobhan packed very lightly, settling for one large
case on wheels that she could pull behind her and a
shoulder bag that would carry the necessities she would
need at hand.

Booking a flight to the West Coast was easy, and the
clerk told her that by the time she reached California,
her overseas flight would be confirmed.

Dazed but determined, she launched her escape, her
mind telling her that it was always better to face things.

She reached Kennedy Airport after numerous snarls
and snags, dragged herself to the proper terminal, barely able to make her lips move in a smile when attendants
spoke to her. Finally they were airborne. Siobhan fell
asleep at once, not even waking when the plane landed
in Chicago to take on more passengers. Then they were
aloft again, racing the sun across a medium-blue sky.

People spoke to her in the terminal in California, and
she assumed that she answered them correctly by the
looks she received.

She slept intermittently on the flight to Australia, ignoring her seatmates.

By the time they flew from Hawaii to the Fiji Islands,
Siobhan was as groggy and disoriented from her self-
imposed isolation as from jet lag.

She landed in Sydney, her lethargy and lassitude an
intolerable burden. She almost didn't care if her mother

met her at the airport or not as she checked her baggage through and turned to find a chair. She might as well curl up in a corner and die.

"Tired, darling?" Jake crooned in her ear, lifting her shoulder bag and pulling the Pullman bag over to one side of the busy, noise-filled terminal.

"Oh, yes, Jake, I'm—" she paused, feeling her mouth fall open as she stared the long way up his frame to his face. "Oh, no! You made the plane make a U-turn and go back to New York! Disgusting plutocrat," she babbled, then looked away from the apparition and stared at the wall. "Siobhan Ryan Butler, get hold of yourself," she said out loud. "In a few minutes, I'll get a cup of herbal tea and then I'll be back to normal."

"I'll get if for you, love," Jake soothed, then leaned down and kissed the top of her head.

"You're not here, you know. I'm perfectly aware that I'm dreaming about you—but I'll deal with it."

"Of course you will." Jake kissed her mouth this time.

It was so enjoyable that she leaned her head way back and opened her lips to him.

"Vona, Vona, is that you?" She heard a familiar voice with just a touch of Aussie drawl.

Siobhan pulled free of the apparition and jumped to her feet. She didn't worry about hitting Jake because she knew that any minute he would disappear. "Mother, oh, mother, I've missed you." She catapulted forward into the warm embrace, loving the feel of her mother's arms around her after so many years.

"Oh, child, child . . . my oldest . . . I've missed you."

"Oh, mama, I needed you so." Siobhan felt the dry sobs tear at her as she hid her face in her mother's neck.

"Vona, my dear. What is it?" There was concern in Sara Selkirk's voice.

"Are you not going to speak to your dad, Vona love?" Andrew whispered.

She lifted her head and blinked at the warmth of Andrew Selkirk, then she disentangled herself from her mother and went into his arms, holding him tight around the neck. "Oh daddy...I missed you. Maura and Lance are fine and Maura is engaged to the finest man—he is so much like you." Siobhan leaned back from him, rubbing her hand across her cheek, then laughing when she saw a tear on Andrew's face.

"Well, I miss my young ones, but I understand that they need to try their wings." He stepped to one side and chuckled when Siobhan jumped in surprise at seeing her brothers Ross, Simon and Jason and her youngest sister, Mary.

There was a babble of conversation and memories as each of the Butlers tried to hug and talk at the same time.

Finally Siobhan noticed that her mother and Andrew were quiet and looking behind her in a questioning way.

"I'm your daughter's fiancé, ma'am, sir. My name is Jake Deerfield."

When the narrow, strong hand came from behind her and into her vision, she whirled around to face Jake. "I thought you were a vision," she hissed. "How did you get here?"

"By plane, my darling, just as you did, but I had better connections." Jake smiled at her family, still speaking to her in low tones.

"No doubt..." Siobhan inhaled, ready to flay him alive.

"She didn't tell us you were accompanying her, Mr. Deerfield," Sara Selkirk said diffidently.

"Please call me Jake, since I'm to be your son-in-law

within a week, right here in Sydney. But to answer your question," Jake said smoothly, not seeming to notice the assorted sounds of surprise around him, "Siobhan wanted to surprise you with our new idea of marrying here in—ouch, darling, I know you want to squeeze me, but mustn't pinch," Jake said mildly, looking down at her.

She almost stepped back, the blue lava of his eyes sending out such menace she was sure the airport alarm would sound any moment. "Ah...we can't marry here." Her mind clattered like an old Remington typewriter. "We were going to honeymoon in—in New York."

"We'll honeymoon at Alice Springs. I have a fancy to backpack to the opal fields too." Jake grinned at the Butlers.

"Backpack? Me?" Siobhan grated, the smile hurting her face. "I'll see you in hell first." She kept her voice low, trying not to make her mother look any more worried.

"Well, we were only going to stay in Sydney one day, then fly back to the station." Andrew looked thoughtful.

"Is there no one there that can look out for things?" Jake inquired.

"Oh yes, there's the foreman, Danby, but you see—"

"Then we're all set," Jake overrode Andrew. "I've booked some suites at the Boulevard Hotel for all of us. My family will be joining us there in a day or two, and of course their friends, the Prentices are coming with—" Jake paused, his smile widening, "—Maura and Lance."

The hubbub of the Butlers rose again like a swirl of leaves in an autumn wind, all of them talking at once and shaking Jake's hand and pummeling his back. Sara

Butler Selkirk had a pink joy in her cheeks while Ross, Simon and Jason were whooping like Indians and Mary had hero worship written all over her as she stared up at Jake. Andrew Selkirk kept nodding and squeezing Sara's hand.

"How dare you seduce my family?" Siobhan said between her teeth as Jake squired her through the terminal to a fleet of cars he had hired, eschewing the use of taxis.

"I have chased you across this planet to marry you, but once we are married, I am going to teach you— Siobhan, my darling—that you can't run from me, that your place is by my side and that if you keep running I'll keep chasing until you finally realize that."

She blinked up at the idling meteor at her side, the twitch of those hard lips the only clue to the hurricane inside the man. "I...I won't be bullied."

"Neither will I. But I won't be separated from you either, even if it means that I have to make all the concessions," Jake said through taut lips. "I don't like being manipulated—by anyone. But I'll learn how to deal with that, too."

"No one manipulates you," Siobhan sputtered, gazing at the Rolls Royces stationed in front of the terminal, then wheeling to face him. "We have nothing in common. Our values are poles apart."

Jake's mouth tightened. "I had the feeling something was wrong when I dropped you at work. Damn you, Siobhan, I told you that we would work things out. We both have to change...." His hands came out to grip her upper arms, heedless of the stares of her family. "We are never parting—not in this life or any other. That is my first vow to you." He led her over to the limousine in which sat her mother and father. He put her into the car none too gently and followed right on her heels. "We are marrying in a small local church."

"How could you work so fast?" she gasped.

"The work was being done while I was flying out here. I have people who know how to cut corners and make things easier for me. If they didn't, I'd get rid of them."

"My parents won't be impressed by plush accommodations or limousines," Siobhan vowed darkly.

Jake looked at her, hard amusement in his face. "They are just like you, are they? I'm hoping when I tell them that my station is located fairly close to theirs, it will please them. Plus, I've made substantial contributions to the Australian Red Cross in both our names, love."

Siobhan looked over her shoulder at her parents in the backseat, smiled, then looked back at Jake. "You're a Svengali—a conniver," she said through her teeth.

"Have you been well, Vona?" Her mother quizzed from the backseat. "You look pale. You used to get such colds when you were a child." Sara pressed her lips together.

When Siobhan opened her mouth to change the subject, Jake was ahead of her. "Tell me more about Siobhan when she was a child."

"Oh," Sara flushed with pleasure. "She was bright and such a hard worker. She always had a job."

"Mother," Siobhan croaked.

"Yes." Jake concurred, his lips on her hair. "She was a very hard worker when I first met her." He took her clenched fists between his two hands, pried them open, then intertwined his fingers with hers.

"It doesn't seem possible that my little girl is getting married," Sara sighed.

"Mrs. Selkirk, it will be just as you want it, I promise." Jake kept a firm hold on Siobhan when she tried to wriggle free.

WHEN THEY arrived at the lovely Boulevard Hotel, the whole Butler clan became a little subdued as they entered. An army of bellhops appeared from nowhere, ready to relieve any burdens.

A man in a morning suit approached Jake and whispered to him. Jake nodded, then turned and took Sara Selkirk's arm and lead her to the elevator.

"I thought you might like to look at some of Max Brainerd's new line. A member of the house will bring them to your suite."

"The designer?" Mary oohed up at a smiling Jake.

"Yes, I thought you might like to look at a few things and see if there was anything that you liked—" His voice trailed off to a murmur as he shepherded both Mary and her mother toward an open elevator.

Andrew put his arm around Siobhan's shoulders. "Taking deep breaths like that, one after the other, could make you faint, love."

"Who does he think he is?" she glared at the closing elevator doors as Andrew led her to another open one. "Intimating that my mother and sister would need special clothes for—"

"Your wedding?" Andrew smiled.

"Yes," she grated, clenching her hands at her sides. "Our family doesn't need his patronizing ways."

"It seems to me that he is doing everything to insure that you marry him this week."

"He's putting on a phony promotion, just to impress you." She was glad of the hand Andrew put under her elbow.

"I know. He told me that he was going to do anything

he had to do to break down any barriers, to wipe out any excuses you might make to postpone the ceremony."

"That's coercion!" Siobhan gulped air as she stepped from the elevator with her stepfather. She looked around her. "Where are the boys?" she quizzed.

"Gone ahead with mother." He touched her cheek with his hand. "You know you are like my own, Siobhan."

"Yes, I know that, darling daddy. You are every bit as dear as my own father was."

"Then tell me that you don't love this man, and nothing he can do will make this marriage take place. Do you love him?"

Siobhan looked up at her stepfather, wanting to tell him that she hated Jake. "He'll want to get rid of me in a year or so, maybe a month or a week." She swiped a finger at the moisture on her cheek, but Andrew's hand with a hankie in it was there first.

"I have my answer, child. Now, you listen to me. You must have a little faith in yourself—in who you are and what you are. I never thought I would see the day when my feisty girl would take a backseat to anyone." Andrew put his arm around her as the elevator doors opened and the liveried bellhop indicated they should alight.

"There are only three suites on this floor, sir and all of them for the Deerfield party. The Prentice family will be one flight above this," the uniformed attendant instructed.

"Thank you," Andrew answered with an innate gentility that made Siobhan quiver with pride.

Such a man my father is, she thought, mulling over his words as they walked in the door of the center suite.

"Andrew—Andrew come see," Sara burbled, clasping her hands, two red spots high on her cheeks. "There's an upstairs and four bedrooms and a sitting room..." she paused for breath, a happy smile on her face. "It's silly to like it so much, I know."

Siobhan stared at the breathless delight of her mother. "See how he breaks people down?" she muttered to her father.

"A very determined man is my son-in-law-to-be, and a little spoiling for your mother is very good for her," Andrew chuckled.

"Twaddle." Siobhan could feel her own mouth turning upward when Mary bounced down the stairs, goggle-eyed, to announce that she could see all of Sydney harbor from her window. "You have cosseted all of us since the moment you met us."

"A wise man grabs a good thing when he sees it. I wanted all of you Butlers for my very own." Andrew kissed the top of Siobhan's head, his gnarled fingers gentle on her cheek. Then he ambled to his wife's side and put his arm around her.

"And do you think you'll like your room, darling?" Jake spoke behind her, making her jump. He kissed her mouth when she turned to him.

"Jake, we should talk. There are so many differences between us." She put her hands on his chest as he drew her close and twisted his body to hide her from the others.

"We will talk—after we marry, and I promise to work out with you any problems we have. But you must promise me that you have stopped running. No more being apart."

Siobhan looked up at him, prepared to argue. Her rebuttal dribbled away like melting wax under the midnight-blue heat of his eyes. "I...I'll make all my vows at the same time."

"Fair enough." Jake watched her, his lashes drooping over his eyes.

She put up her hand, and touched his mouth. "Jake, I think we should talk before our marriage, too. There are certain things that I want—just as I'm sure there are factors important to you."

"Do you want a contract? A legal document?"

She hesitated, then nodded. "That might be best."

"I'll have my lawyer here in Sydney—"

"You have a lawyer in Sydney?" she looked up at him again.

"I have an international corporation, Siobhan," he said, thin-lipped. "You will be a very wealthy woman in your own right." He strode across the room to her parents, directing their attention out the suite window.

Siobhan stood there swallowing, words tossed in her mind like loose ball bearings. Nothing came together!

"Vona...Vona..." Mary called to her, waving her up the stairs, eyes snapping with excitement.

As she followed her sister up the stairs, the phone rang. She paused on the stairs to watch Jake grab up the instrument and bark into it.

"What? Alastair Nivens? From Max's? Right. Send him up." Jake banged down the phone, looking with narrowed eyes at Siobhan for a second, then back to her mother. "A man named Alastair Nivens is coming up and bringing some samples and gowns from Max's for you ladies to see."

"I'll die..." Mary breathed, hanging over the balcony on the second-floor landing.

"You will if you don't stop hanging on that railing," Andrew said, smiling at his saucer-eyed stepdaughter.

"I think we should leave, Andrew—and find other diversions." Jake gave a grim laugh.

Unexpected pain gripped Siobhan. He would go downstairs and flirt with a barmaid! He would find a beautiful bare-breasted Australian woman at Bondi Beach and run off with her!

She turned and went up the rest of the stairs to the second level.

"Why are you coming up now, Vona?" Mary looked at her in mild wonder. "Do you have a headache? Your eyes look so glassy."

"Headache? Why not?" she mumbled, staring straight ahead and walking toward an open door.

"Boy!" Mary took hold of her arm and turned her around just as the suite bell rang. "I hope I'm not this dippy when it comes time for me to marry."

"Mary, you are a cruel person," Siobhan mumbled as her sister left at the top of the stairs and galloped to open the door with a breathless "Hi".

The first minutes after Nivens's arrival were blurry for Siobhan as her mind followed Jake out of the suite and down the elevator to the lobby, where he happened on a gorgeous redhead in a see-through outfit that drove him wild. Then he. . . .

"Vona. . .darling, pay attention. Mr. Nivens seems to think that pearl gray would go with my coloring. What do you think?" Sara stared at her daughter with a mixture of concern and puzzlement.

Siobhan shook herself mentally and stared at her mother's silver-gray wavy hair, her deep violet eyes that were like her daughter's and the tall, slightly heavy but graceful, figure. She blinked a few times. "Yes. Pearl-gray silk with the amethysts that Andrew gave you. . . ."

Her mother was nodding excitedly.

"And I do happen to have shoes and a bag in violet leather since we were told that you had violet eyes, Mrs. Selkirk." Alastair waved to a helper who rummaged through a case at his feet, bringing out the accessories with a flourish.

"Is it customary for you to come to a hotel supplied with clothing and accoutrements?" Siobhan asked in a faint voice as she watched others unpack cases. They began to twist and turn a delighted Mary as they pinned, sewed and fitted.

Alastair Nivens's eyes twinkled. "On rare occasions we do this. Usually when it's damn the expense."

Siobhan gave a weak laugh as her mother and sister chuckled gleefully.

"Now, Mr. Deerfield said your wedding dress would be arriving tomorrow but you'd still need other clothing plus a full complement of camping gear—for Alice Springs and the opal fields. You are quite a hardy soul, I must say, Miss Butler."

"But he was only teasing about that, surely." Siobhan gaped at the khaki clothing and boots brought out by an attendant who proceeded to describe the use of each piece he displayed.

"That's it, then. He intends to murder me when we're in the outback." Siobhan delivered this well-enunciated speech to her stunned listeners.

"Vona, for heaven's sake! What are you saying?"

"She's bonkers," Mary breathed.

"And you are a most unkind child." Siobhan staggered to her feet and lifted her chin. "Go ahead, Mr. Nivens, outfit me. 'We who are about to die salute you.'"

9

WITH THE ARRIVAL two days later of the Deerfield family and the Prentices, the pre-nuptial celebration shifted into high gear. Siobhan had the sensation of free-falling through a hurricane.

Jake had met them all at the airport and then driven them back to the hotel to rest.

Now, as Siobhan watched her impatient sister Mary put the last touches to her makeup, she couldn't be sorry that all the Butlers were reunited after such a long separation. Even with that, she dreaded the evening—and dreaded even more the next day, when she would marry Jake.

"Vona, stop mooning in the mirror like that. Jake said we have to be on time for the rehearsal, and that after we have dinner we're going to a disco and then..." Mary babbled almost out of breath.

"Are mother and Maura downstairs?" She smiled at her sister, then stood up to twitch at her dress.

"Yes, they've been talking nonstop. Mama loves your mother-in-law—she came up here while you were napping. Wow, Vona, that dress is gorgeous. Is that color peach?" Mary stopped the avalanche of words to haul in a deep breath.

"Apricot satin," Siobhan said hesitating, wondering what her mother and Andrew would think of the strapless satin that came up to her knee in front, gathered at the waist and bodice very tightly, then swept back into a bustle and a mini-train. If so much of her breasts wasn't showing it could almost have been a demure style. Her hair was twisted on top of her head in a cone, a coronet of apricot-colored tea roses from Jake her only adornment. Her marquise-shaped emerald was back on her finger, and in her ears she wore new earrings also supplied by Jake. Siobhan put up her hand to the string of three flawless emeralds set in apricot enamel, the curving shape just fitting the outer edge of her ear.

"You look marvelous, Vona. So do I," Mary giggled, standing next to her sister and looking in the mirror. "I like this blue eyelet dress Alastair made me."

"Conceited, aren't you?"

The door pushed open, and Jake stood there, his eyes on Siobhan. He hardly seemed to notice when Mary danced around him and out the room. "You're too beautiful—but you always were, even in your waitress dress and apron." Jake shook his head, his eyes a simmering blue heat. "I don't know how that priest will keep his mind on the rehearsal, but if he so much as looks at you—" Jake stared at her, entranced. "Do you have a wrap?" he asked suddenly.

"Yes." She went to the bed and leaned down to fetch her wrap. Jake's arm reached around her, his other hand settling at her waist. "We're driving together. The others have already gone, I'm sure."

"Mary?"

"Gone with the others. Will it smear your lip gloss if I kiss you?"

His face was so close to hers that she could see the golden streaks in his blue eyes. "No. It's smearproof." She tried to clear the hoarseness from her throat.

"Darling, what a clever idea," Jake muttered, his

mouth closing on hers, his tongue in gentle pressure against hers.

The kiss lengthened and deepened. Siobhan dropped her clutch purse and gripped Jake's waist, her body pushing closer to him.

"Love, we had better go now, I think." Jake inhaled a shaky breath. "I still haven't forgiven you for running from me, and we're going to talk about it."

"Oh?" She lifted her chin.

"Relax, darling." Jake nuzzled her hair for a moment before lifting his head to gaze at her, the slow molten heat of his eyes swirling around her.

Her reactions slowed to zero when she was this close to Jake. "We'll be late," she whispered as his face drifted nearer.

"Yes." His lips touched hers, lifted, touched again. Then he sighed and straightened. "Come along, wife, it's time to go."

All the raw feelings that lay submerged surfaced in a tidal wave. "You don't have to go through with this," she huffed stiffening.

He looked down at her, grinning. "Darling, you're as touchy as I am. We can hurt each other, can't we?"

Siobhan watched him for long seconds, then nodded.

"Let's go, sweetheart. We'll talk another time."

The ride through Sydney at night was awesome. "I didn't expect it to be so wonderful," Siobhan gasped.

Jake laughed. "Australia is all wild contrasts. The opera house here is second to none in the world and the desert is as wild and fearsome as anywhere on the planet."

She settled back in the cushioned comfort of the bucket seat. "The people are marvelous..." Siobhan sighed. "Your family is great, too...but...."

"Why do I get the feeling that my bride is hesitating?" Jake didn't look at her as he turned the wheel and swung the car into the parking area of a small Gothic-style church. Jake pulled on the hand brake and turned to face her, his left arm resting on the wheel. "Well, do you like the traditional church I've found for us?"

Siobhan wanted to laugh at him. *I would have married you if Pinocchio was to be the minister, James Kendall, darling,* she shouted in the silence of her mind. "It'll do," she answered tartly.

Scowling, Jake pushed open his door and came around the front of the car to help her from her seat.

Siobhan, standing next to him, sensed the volatile change in him. Inflammable chemicals boomed through his system. She knew she had better run.

"Jake...is that you Jake? What the blazes is holding you up? Everyone is here." David Deerfield strode toward their car, even the deepening twilight did not mask his scowl. "You know damn well how your mother badgers me when this type of thing doesn't go off on time...." He stopped a few feet from them, his eyes needling between his son and Siobhan. "What's going on?"

"Nothing." Jake spat the word into the night sky then propelled Siobhan ahead of him toward the church.

"Release me at once," she grated, her voice low, as David Deerfield trotted behind them.

"No, damn you, I won't release you," Jake barked back.

They sailed up the steps and through the arched oak doors, her heels clattering as Jake took her at a run down the center aisle. "Stop it," she hissed, watching her brothers and sisters look at her with gaping mouths.

"Vona does the weirdest things," Mary remarked absently, her voice rising like a carillon in the Gothic structure.

Before Siobhan could speak a formal-sounding cough stopped her in her tracks.

"I am Father Colvin of St. Catherine's. Could we start the rehearsal?"

She opened her mouth to tell him that she wasn't about to take part in the Great Charade of the Century, when Jake stepped forward and kissed her full on the mouth, paralyzing her and making the families titter and groan behind them.

"We are ready, Father. Go ahead."

On their way out, Siobhan was taken aback when David said he planned spending a week on the station before returning to the United States.

"Your problem is that you are a snob, my darling," grinned Jake. "My father worked as a stevedore when he was a young man, and spent two years as a cowboy in Montana before he finished college."

Siobhan looked up at him as they left the church behind the others. "And did you do all those things?"

"It's about time you asked those questions. Yes. I was a rodeo rider for a time, and I even took part in the Calgary Stampede."

"You did not." Siobhan stopped and stared at him.

"Yes, I did. Isn't it about time that Mr. and Mrs. Deerfield exchanged a few confidences?"

"I'm not Mrs. Deerfield yet." A thought struck her like a velvet fist. "Perhaps I should keep my own name."

"As you wish," Jake spoke between his teeth. "My lawyer will be at dinner with us. Len Barrymore is a very shrewd individual and I have told him that you are to have your wishes in this contract."

"Even if I choose to see him alone?"

"Yes," he threw back icily.

The doors closed behind them with a muted boom, the excited chatter of the others drifting back to them from the parking lot as they hurried to the cars.

"Do you know the way, Jake?" David called to him.

"Yes," Jake raised his voice to answer.

They walked without speaking to the car, Jake's hand heavy on her arm.

Siobhan spent the trip through town gazing out her window at the Sydney night. Wherever she looked there were people walking, talking, laughing, their clothes as varied as New Yorkers'. Jeans marched with gowns, party pants with skirts and evening jackets.

When they at last drove into a well-lit parking area and stopped, Siobhan had the feeling that there was no escape from her fate.

The restaurant had a gilt-edged approach to its guests that told her more than words that this was the soda bar for the crème de la crème of Sydney.

"Don't you know any folksy places where people just eat food? Where they don't sit around waiting to be placed in the London or New York *Times*?"

A muscle twitched in Jake's face. "I assumed that you would want your family to have the best food to be found in Sydney. Michel's has that reputation."

Siobhan swallowed. "Sorry. That was bitchy."

"Kind of you to admit it," Jake growled, then led her to a table. "I want you to meet Len Barrymore."

When Jake introduced her to the lawyer, Siobhan felt her face give way to a smile. She liked his rough-hewn face and warm handshake.

"Miss Butler, I am most happy to meet you. Anyone who can catch the elusive Jake Deerfield must be one sharp lady." He turned to look at Jake. "This was a good idea, having the dinner in the private dining area. It makes it easier to converse with everyone."

Jake leaned down and kissed Siobhan's cheek. "I'll join mother, who's waving to me, and you can tell Len just what it is that you want in our contract." He strode across the room without looking back.

Siobhan couldn't help but notice how the dinner jacket of deep green silk fit Jake's shoulders.

"I suppose I could just stand here and say nothing while you stare after Jake, but I'm not the long-suffering type," Len drawled.

Siobhan wheeled to face him, feeling her face redden. "Sorry. I didn't mean to be rude."

"You weren't. I'm jealous because a beautiful woman like you has never looked at me like that—with so much love in her eyes."

Their table was situated so that they could not only hear the musicians but see them as well. "Now tell me what it is you would like included in this contract that both you and Jake will be signing?"

"Must he see it?"

Len leaned back from her, his brow furrowed. "I would never let a client sign something that he had not read or that I had not explained to him."

Siobhan nodded, then licked her dry lips before speaking. "I want a clause stating that he will never leave me until we have exhausted every avenue there is to reconciliation."

"And of course Jake is to have the same premise in his contract?"

She blinked up at the lawyer. "That isn't necessary. I would never want to leave Jake."

Len hesitated with his pen in the air. "How is Jake to know that?"

"I...I suppose you could put it in for both of us." She sipped her white wine greedily, feeling thirsty and disoriented.

Len cleared his throat, tapping at the top of the gold pen that fitted into the small brown-lizard writing case he was using. "Jake said something about you wanting to retain your own name. This is not unusual and requires no special legal actions."

"I want to take Jake's name."

"Are there many things that you need to discuss with each other before I declare this a legal document?"

"Yes. I want it clearly stated that in case of divorce or dissolution of marriage, if I am still working, there will be no alimony of any kind. If I am not working, there will be financial support only until I find employment."

"I see." Len's face didn't look as though he "saw" at all. He studied her in puzzlement.

"I really don't want Jake's money," Siobhan smiled at him, not caring if he believed her or not. "I make a substantial salary at the present time, and I think I could always find work."

"You are one beautiful lady, Siobhan Butler," Len shook his head. "I wish I'd met you first."

She could have told him that it wouldn't have made any difference if she had met Jake for the first time today or fifteen years ago, but she only smiled.

"In all fairness, I should point out that Jake's money is in the mucho class and that he is a generous man."

"I want the contract to read as I said, please."

"Of course. But if you ever do decide to leave Jake, will you come to Australia so that I—"

"Is that ethical?" Jake's voice chopped between them making Siobhan's glass jump in her hand.

Len Barrymore looked around at the other man, not noticeably ruffled. "Maybe not."

"Darling," Jake spoke in a precise way, not taking his eyes off Len. "Dinner is about to be served and we are sitting with our parents."

"Of course." Siobhan reached for another glass of champagne as a waiter passed, putting her empty down on the tray.

"I thought you didn't drink," Jake crooned.

"New hobby," she answered, gulping most of the liquid as she walked at Jake's side. She smiled at the foursome already seated at the round table.

"Sit down here, dear, between your mother and me," Jess Deerfield patted the seat.

"No," Jake barked. "She is sitting with me."

"Really, Jake . . ." his mother's face creased in a frown. "Must you always be a bear?"

"I am tired of Siobhan always being taken from me. I want her next to me," Jake informed his mother.

"Right you are," Andrew supported him. "I have always wanted my Sara by my side."

David Deerfield looked at his son and shook his head, smiling. "I've never seen him like this." He looked up as Jake held Siobhan's chair for her. "I can hear your teeth grinding from here."

"Can you?" Jake bared his teeth when his father guffawed.

"Really, James Kendall, you might try to be civil in front of your in-laws. Oh, dear there's Patricia. Darling, over here, and dear Edmund, too. I wonder if they brought the children. . . ."

"Lord, I hope not." Jake uncurled his body from his

seat and turned to embrace the diminutive brunette who flung herself at him.

"I heard that Jake, you louse, and for two cents I'd call home and have the three of them shipped here." Patricia Campbell leaned back in her brother's arms, threw a kiss to her parents and darted her eyes around the table, fixing at last on Siobhan. "Ah, you must be the one, you gorgeous thing. What did you use for bait to catch this brother of mine."

"Raw shark meat," Siobhan said in low tones.

Patricia tittered and repeated Siobhan's reply to her husband, Ed Campbell, who had come up behind her to wring Jake's hand.

"Good—she's a fighter. I wouldn't have thought there was a woman who would go back at you, Jake." Patricia pushed around her brother and held out her hands to Siobhan who rose from her chair to take them. "Sweet mother of the prophet, she's an Amazon."

Siobhan laughed and squeezed the hands she held, then she turned to be embraced by Edmund.

It took some minutes for all the greetings and introductions to be finished, but by the time Siobhan resumed her seat, she felt very comfortable with the newly arrived members of Jake's family.

"Did you think I would let that slide by?" Jake leaned over and whispered in her ear, his arm on the back of her chair.

"What?" Siobhan didn't turn her head, knowing that she would be nose-to-nose with him if she did.

"The remark about raw shark meat, my treasure," Jake hissed, his breath entering her ear.

"Have you no sense of humor?"

"Oh yes, I do, otherwise I would have retaliated years

ago," Jake said in soothing tones, his finger wrapping and unwrapping one of her curls around it.

"Primitive."

"Good. You're beginning to learn."

She inhaled a deep breath and faced him, her lips coming to rest on his chin. She nipped it with her teeth. "You don't scare me, buster."

"Scaring you is the last thing I want to do, but I do want you to know that I'm not giving you up to anyone or anything." Jake was interrupted by his sister calling to him. Grim-faced, he looked away from Siobhan.

"But you'll probably toss me away some day," she mumbled into her tulip-shaped glass as Hughy Prentice rose to give a toast.

"To one of the most admirable persons I know, a woman of strength, beauty and purpose. To Siobhan," Hughy said. All the guests surged to their feet, glasses raised.

Jake unfolded slowly from his chair, his eyes never leaving her face as he lifted his glass, then emptied it.

Hughy waited until glasses were refilled and the guests had reseated themselves, then he hoisted his glass again. "And to my best friend, who was so attracted to the star of 'Day By Day', but who fell in love with a waitress in a diner." Hughy chortled and drank from his glass, then proceeded to explain to the Australian guests what he meant by the two toasts.

Siobhan ignored the buzzing murmurs and laughter of the others and stared at Jake. His face was like a teakwood carving, with one muscle quivering at the corner of his mouth, a dark crimson moving up his neck.

Without thinking, she reached out and put her hand on the muscle spasm, the index finger in velvet pressure there. "You mustn't mind Hughy. He sees romance in everything since he and Maura decided to marry. I know you weren't in love with Vona Butler the waitress."

Jake shifted in his chair so that his body was between her and the others. "You know nothing." The hiss of his words was like steam between them.

Siobhan stared at him, feeling surrounded by an electrical charge. "Jake, I...."

"Hey, you two," Lance called. "Andrew is going to make a toast now."

Andrew made his toast but Siobhan could not have said what it was. There was a buzzing in her ears, a pounding in her blood, that blanked out her senses, deafened her, blinded her to those around her. What had Jake meant? What was he saying?

"Shall we dance?"

"What?" she looked around her blinking. "Yes, I'd like to dance."

"You're a beautiful dancer, Siobhan. Did you dance much when we were apart?" Jake guided with the flat of his hand on her spine. Then, as they walked together onto the floor, he turned her into his arms. "You look beautiful tonight. Your clothes sense is so perfect. I wouldn't give a damn if you wore spats and jeans, but I still love to watch you walk toward me dressed so well." He swung her out from his body, grinning at her. "Of course, you realize that nothing you ever buy will ever affect me as much as the outfit you wore the night we became engaged...."

She felt laughter bubble inside her. It was so free and lovely to dance with Jake. "I doubt you will ever see that ensemble again. I only took it on loan from Chouchou."

Jake stopped in the middle of the floor, holding her

close to him. "Is that right? I'll have to see about that."

She smiled at him. "Don't be silly." Then she wiggled her hips at him, chuckling when his eyes dropped at once to her body. "Dance with me, mad impetuous fool. Tomorrow you'll be married and your wife probably won't let you out of the house."

Jake's smile went over her like velvet. "Is that right? Well, then, pretty lady, let the good times roll."

Suddenly, Siobhan felt something release her feet and ankles as though she had been tied to earth since she was born and now Jake had set her free. She was unbonded. She would give herself to Jake tomorrow.

Music entered her soul and she and Jake became one in the throbbing cadence.

"Darling, I think we're making, love." Jake gave a shaky laugh in her ear.

"Of course." She let her fingers run through his hair, mussing it. "Did I tell you that I like your nose? It has a little bump almost at the top, but mostly it's very straight and strong. Strong noses are important."

"Are they?" Jake chuckled.

"Yes..." Siobhan leaned back from him but didn't loosen her clasp around his neck. "Did you ever see a successful diplomat with a turned-up nose? No. Did you ever see a professional football player with a little one? Of course not. You see?"

"You're crackers, lady mine." Jake moved well to the soft rock and roll. "That is one sexy beat."

"Isn't it? I love it."

"It shows." He reached for her and pulled her close to him once more.

"I don't think we should be dancing so close to this beat." She smiled up at him. "You have the thickest eyelashes for a man—"

Jake's grin had a twist to it as he looked down at her. "You say the craziest things, and you're so damned changeable. One minute you won't speak to me, the next you're chattering about anything and everything." He shook his head. "I wish I'd married you years ago. I've missed some beautiful years with you."

10

SYDNEY PUT ON its best party dress for the wedding. The sunny sky was dotted here and there with fleecy clouds; the flowers and foliage had the soft fresh sheen that an overnight rain bestows.

"How come you're not nervous, sis? Mama and Maura are falling apart," Mary informed her with great relish.

"Monster," Siobhan murmured as she stepped into the ecru satin slip that was in itself a strapless dress. It was tightly fitted over the bodice and fell in soft folds to her ankles. She wrapped a makeup cape around her shoulders to put the last touches to a feathering of base, blusher and lavender eye shadow.

"You know, I don't ever remember you being beautiful when we lived in the States," Mary mused as she pulled a chair up next to Siobhan, now seated in front of the mirror. "Your hair was bloody awful."

"If Andrew hears you talking like a street urchin he's liable to paddle you," Siobhan studied her sister in the mirror, trying to look stern, her hand poised with the shadow brush in it. "I must say you look smashing in that pale green you're wearing."

"Yes, I do, don't I. Unlike you and Maura, I'm not going to go through an ugly stage."

Siobhan smiled at her sister, completed her makeup, then stood, removing the cape and putting it away.

Slowly, she approached the clothes tree that held pride of place in the room.

The door opened just as she was taking down the dress.

"Oh, good. Mother and I came to help you dress," Maura said, a quaver in her voice.

Sara Selkirk stood there staring at her daughter, blinking and biting her lip.

Siobhan blessed the presence of her mother and sisters in the next hour because she had to work so hard to distract them that she was unable to keep track of the passing time.

By the time Andrew knocked on the door, the four of them were ready. He walked in with a package in his hands. "This is for you, Siobhan love, from Jake."

She opened the jewelry case and stared at the diamonds lying on pink satin. "It's the most beautiful necklace I have ever seen. Mother, look at the lavender enamel chain," she breathed.

"Jake told me that the stones belonged to his maternal grandmother and that he had a designer in New York do the enameling to match your eyes." Andrew grinned as the women oohed and aahed.

Siobhan clutched the box in her hands as her mother fastened the necklace for her. *Why didn't you give me this yourself, Jake,* Siobhan screamed at him in her mind. *Why did you give this to Andrew to. . . .*

"Vona? Are you daydreaming, love?" Andrew patted her on the shoulder. "It's time for us to go. The others are being driven by Hughy. Len Barrymore is going to drive us."

"Lovely." She swallowed and took the arm of the man who was a father to her. "This day means so much because you're giving me away, daddy. Thank you."

Andrew patted the hand resting on his arm, his eyes moist as he stared at her. "You are so beautiful, my dear child. That dress is so old-world with the high neck and the long sleeves. You look like a very tall, very slender Queen Victoria in ecru silk. Even the train is elegant. Can a train be elegant?" Andrew quizzed her. "I see the wetness in your eyes that I feel in mine. I think we had better go before we ruin your makeup."

"The rat-tat-tat you hear is my knees," she informed him as they descended the stairs of the apartment to the main level.

"That rumble you hear is a father's protest about giving up his first-born," Andrew whispered as Len Barrymore rose and came toward them.

"Siobhan, you are so beautiful. Is that a silk rose that your veil is attached to, or is it real?" Len kissed her hand, then her cheek.

"It's silk." She smiled at him, feeling some of the seasickness leave her.

"You look like a goddess, and your veil is like a waterfall," Len said, then laughed. "I never thought I'd get lyrical."

Andrew looked at his watch. "It's time to go."

The ride to the church was too short for her, yet something made her want to scream at the driver to speed up.

The church had the luster of moonstone, its oaken doors standing open like welcoming arms.

They entered the church to be surrounded at once by the family.

Sara hugged her daughter, and gulped great breaths before Ross eased her free and, as one of the ushers, led his mother down the aisle.

"I will never understand how Jake did all this—

flowers, tuxes..." Siobhan muttered as she took her father's arm and they began their slow march to the altar.

Father Colvin was a clear, concise speaker whose deep voice penetrated to the last pew, but Siobhan had to try and read his lips. Her hearing went, her vision was blurry, her body began to numb starting with the toes. Yet she felt Jake's pulse, every breath he took, each nuance in his voice.

Jake turned her to face him, then let his lips descend gently on hers.

"Is it over?" she whispered.

He chuckled and nodded.

"Are we married?"

"Very."

She turned back to Father Colvin. "Thank you very much. I enjoyed it." She didn't know why Jake was laughing but it seemed a welcome addendum to the recessional music.

The reception was in the Boulevard Hotel and Siobhan had a good time there, too. In fact, when Jake told her they should get ready to go, she balked. "Why? Aren't we staying in Sydney tonight?"

"No, darling, we're flying out in a private plane to a camping site owned by a friend of Len Barrymore's, not too far from the Warrego River. I thought we'd dig for opals for a while."

"You're fooling me. Right?"

"Wrong." Jake kissed her forehead, then looked past her and smiled. "Ah, here's Maura to help you change. See you in about fifteen minutes."

She talked to herself all the time Maura was helping her into a khaki skirt and sensible shoes for the flight. In the Ferrari next to Jake, she turned to look at him. "I don't know anything about digging opals."

"You'll learn."

"Instead of candlelight and wine, we'll have Coleman lanterns and warm Australian beer."

"Oh, I think the cooler will keep the beer chilled."

They drove onto an airfield, where Jake stopped the car and directed a man to load their luggage onto a sleek airplane, its engine already running.

"I didn't expect a jet," Siobhan murmured as she climbed on board with Jake's help, turning toward the cabin.

"Come and sit up here and keep me company," Jake smiled at her as he sat down in the pilot's seat and strapped on a headset, gesturing for her to do the same. Then he fastened both seat belts and they were taxiing down the field.

"You don't fly . . ."

"Yes, I do, love. Let go of my arm. That's better."

Siobhan kept her eyes open on takeoff because all her muscles seemed to have atrophied and her eyelids wouldn't move.

Her initial fear faded in the beauty of the land they were flying over, and though the noise was not so bad that it would prevent conversation, she was too taken with the green hills and the blue sky to say anything.

She had no idea of the time because she was so engrossed in the landscape below, but as Jake began his descent she felt a rebirth of tension. The landing field was only a strip on a pasture but Jake set the plane down smoothly.

From the air, Siobhan had seen a sprawling house with a wraparound porch and some outbuildings, but once on the ground, grassy knolls hid the buildings from view.

"Not to worry, wife of mine, there's a jeep parked

over there in that shed." Jake pointed as they climbed out of the plane. "I'll be right back." He left her standing in the shade cast by the plane and jogged to the shed.

She heard the cough and sputter of a motor, and then the jeep was roaring toward her, stopping with a screech of brakes and puffs of dirt rising around them. She helped Jake stow the lighter grips in the vehicle, then climbed in on her side. They went bouncing down a dirt road that took them over several grassy humps, then down to a flat piece of ground where the house, grayed by age and weather, waited for them. The windows glittered at them sightlessly, no person appearing on the huge veranda that waisted the dwelling.

"Will your friend mind that we're staying here? Will we interfere with the working of his station?" Siobhan asked in a low voice as they stopped in front of the house.

"The station manager lives over the hill. His wife and mother clean this house, but we will be virtually on our own." Jake hefted most of the luggage onto the porch, then took a key from the top of the door frame and opened the door. "Come here, Mrs. Deerfield." He swept her up into his arms and carried her into the house. "Welcome to your first home, my darling. The owner of this station is carrying you in his arms."

She stared at Jake as he let her slide down his body. "Are there really opals nearby?"

"Oh yes, that part is true. But do you think we'll have the time or the inclination to search for opals?" Jake grinned at her, then went out to bring in the rest of the baggage. He paused at the foot of the stairs, a grip in each hand, motioning to her to precede him. "Mrs. Deerfield," his voice rose around her like a velvet wrap, "we are finally going to have that talk we should have had two years ago."

Siobhan felt a fluttering all through her as they unpacked. Each time she looked over at Jake, he was looking at her.

She closed the drawer on the oak bureau and turned almost into Jake's arms.

He stood there, staring down at her, then he inhaled deeply and spoke. "I wanted you badly the first time I ever saw you, when you were galloping around that diner doing the work of three men." Jake took her hand and led her out of the room and down the stairs in the air-conditioned coolness. "I didn't look down on you because you were a waitress, Siobhan. That wasn't why I fought against you. It was because when you said 'May I take your order?' I damn well almost said, 'Will you marry me?' That shook me to my shoes. I wanted to avoid you like the plague. I sure as hell never intended to see you again."

Jake didn't release her hand even when he opened the refrigerator in the kitchen and lifted out a cold beer and a mineral water. Her hand was still in his when he took the bottle opener from the drawer. "I'm not letting you go, so you'll have to hold the bottles while I work the opener."

"You're silly," Siobhan giggled, feeling happiness bubble like the mineral water she was drinking, because Jake was hers. "I thought I disgusted you because—"

"I looked for reasons to dislike you, Siobhan—to find fault with you. I needed time to think, to figure out what had happened to me," Jake kissed her cheek.

"You thought I was a cheap whore," Siobhan swallowed, gasping when his fingers dug into her side.

"No!" he thundered, slamming the glass bottle down.

He didn't seem to notice that it shattered, spilling its contents on the counter, glass shooting across the formica.

"Your hand—you've cut it." She took his between her own, lifting it to her mouth and sucking gently.

"Huh? Oh. It's only a scratch. Not that I want you to stop what you're doing." Jake leaned over her, kissing the top of her head. "But I still want you to listen to me. I did a great many things that were stupid, but I swear to you, when we made love, I was committed to you from that moment. There was no turning back for me. My life was yours and I was determined to make you see that we belonged together. When I left you at the diner that day, I went back to Deerfield Hall, dictated a week's work to my secretary and had my assistant reschedule all my meetings. I had no intention of leaving your side until I'd convinced you that we belonged together. That night when I couldn't find you—" Jake's face suddenly turned ashen. "When Clarence said you'd left the area...." His voice hoarsened, as they made their way from the kitchen to the lounge.

"I looked everywhere for you. When I went back to New York, I asked Hughy about you, what he knew..." Jake ground out.

"I told him to tell you nothing," Siobhan crooned, settling herself more comfortably against him, sighing when his hand moved up under her breast.

"If you keep wriggling like that, wife of mine, we'll never get this story told," Jake muttered, a flush of red lacing his jawbone.

She responded by nibbling at his chin. "You're mine, for real, aren't you? It isn't just a wish—something I dreamed?"

"I'm yours, my angel. I have been right along. But it's

been one tough road." He kissed her eyes. "Now talk to me."

"It was very hard at first, in New York. I used to wake up, thinking you were holding me." She tightened her hands on his neck. "I tried very hard to forget you, and hard work helped. Hughy was my friend. There was never anything else between us. I paid back every cent of the money he loaned me for my education."

The muscle jumped near Jake's mouth. "I was damned jealous of him, especially when I learned that you lived in an apartment house that he owned. I could have killed him. I would kill anyone who tried to take you from me." His eyes fixed on hers. "If you ever leave me, I'm a dead man—even though I might keep moving, eating, sleeping, maybe even having sex—"

"Oh, no, you won't." Siobhan grabbed his ears and brought his face closer to hers.

"—having business meetings, dancing, whatever. Without you, I'll be a zombie. There you have it, sweetheart, complete control. How does it feel?"

"It's only justice." She grinned at him, feeling helium-light. "You've had me the same length of time, the same way. Now we have each other, forever."

Jake cuddled her to him, his hand moving up her thigh and squeezing gently.

"We'll have terrible fights. Our words are bound to hurt now and then." She felt a painful tingling in her limbs at the thought of being estranged from Jake.

"Then let's set some ground rules. Let's settle the grievances as they come. Cardinal rule number one: we always talk to each other. Rule number two: we never part or go to sleep angry."

Siobhan looked down at him. "I really do love you

very much, you know. I'm very clumsy with you," she grimaced.

Jake's coloring fluctuated from pasty white to brick red. "I love you too—and it hurts like hell sometimes." He gave her a lopsided grin. "But you're not clumsy with me—just changeable. You disappear into the landscape, then appear like a summer rose. Chameleon, my chameleon love." He shook his head, then nuzzled her cheek. "If I don't keep my eye on you, you could vanish again, and I couldn't take that. Now, I have a very strong urge to show you the bedroom." He grinned at her. "I've made you blush again. I like doing that. Was it because I mentioned the bedroom?"

"No, it was because you read my mind," Siobhan laughed, feeling the years of tension melt away. She stopped when they were halfway up the stairs, facing him. "Just think—we can make love, fall asleep, and when we wake up, we'll be together."

"Siobhan, my darling, where did you get the idea that you would be sleeping?"

Their laughter trailed behind them as they entered the bedroom.

"Jake, it's lovely. Everything blue and cream . . ." she smiled at him in question.

He shrugged. "Yes, I did have the master suite done over when I knew I had to follow you out to Australia." The flash of hurt on his face almost escaped her. "It isn't bad for a rush job."

"I ran out of fear, Jake—fear that you wouldn't want me after a while." She waved her arms, watching his eyes fix on her breasts and feeling her body arch in response, as though all the modeling and acting she had ever done were for this moment. "I should be ashamed of myself, but I want you to look at me and admire me. I want you to be proud of my body."

"Not just your body, my angel. I desire your mind, the core of you, your essence." Jake closed his eyes. "Stop digressing with your form, wife, I'm hyped enough, or haven't you noticed?"

"I've noticed." Siobhan patted his chest, loving it when he sucked in his breath. "It is so lovely to have power."

"I can never keep you to the point. You're always jumping here, then there, changing moods—"

"And colors, like a chameleon."

"You were saying why you ran from me," Jake slid the zipper of her khaki skirt downward.

"Are you going to be my valet?"

"Yes."

"Thank you. Now, let's see. Why did I run from you?" She could feel the scowl on her face. "It seems so silly now—to run from the person who gives you life. But the overpowering fear of having and then losing you drove me away. It was a recurring nightmare to me." She smiled at him as he unbuttoned her blouse. She felt drugged with love. "I think at this moment I could have a wisdom tooth pulled and not blink."

Jake's eyes narrowed on her for a moment. "It can't be the champagne. You didn't have enough."

"Oh, yes I did. But it isn't the wine. It's just being here, being undressed by you." She blinked at a painful memory.

Jake touched her lip with his index finger. "You're remembering when I took off your bra that first time we made love. It had been mended, but it was clean. That's what you told me." Jake smiled at her, before leaning down to kiss one of her nipples. "I didn't see the bra, even when you mentioned it. All I could see was that skin, like a pink pearl. I wanted to kiss every centimeter of it."

"I think you did." She inhaled a shaky laugh, loving the heat building in her body for Jake.

"Yes, I did, didn't I?" The smile came and went.

Jake sat her down on the bed and removed her sandals. Then he held her cool, bare feet in his hands, kissing each toe. "Even your toes are graceful, wife."

"I have a corn." She bent forward and pointed to her little toe. "I wore too-tight shoes in one segment of the show."

Jake looked up and laughed, his amusement touched with passion. "No artifice at all, is there, Siobhan Ryan Butler Deerfield?"

"Well, I wouldn't want you to think you had a wife without flaws." She leaned toward him as he gently dropped her feet and began to kiss her knees. She stroked his black, almost curling hair, lightly grazing her skin with its wiry softness, an erotic experience that she wanted to repeat over and over again.

"Too late. You may be marred in the eyes of others, my angel, but to me you are perfect." He stretched his neck and their lips met in soft covenant, then he sat beside her on the bed holding her hand, both of them naked. "Do you remember that night Hughy brought you to the restaurant so we could meet?"

"Yes. I was terrified. I was sure that you would recognize me at once and throw me through a window." She rubbed her shoulder against his arm.

"I turned around and looked at you—at your eyes that were so like Vona Butler's—and I panicked. I thought the similarity was in my mind. I damned you, Siobhan Ryan, and I damned Vona Butler who still had a power over me."

"Was that why you attacked me?"

"Probably. I couldn't see anything clearly. There I was, floored by television's sexy Raine, and thinking of a waitress in a diner, at the same time. That evening I could easily have been certified." He put his arm around her, his fingers skimming her waist. "You have silky skin, Mrs. Deerfield."

"Thank you." Siobhan looked up at him, realizing she must have a silly look on her face. She didn't care. It felt so good to be with Jake, to talk with him, to know that they were going to be together for all time. She straightened as a thought struck her. Before she could move any further, Jake caught her close to him again. She grinned up at him, then put her finger on his lips to stop him from kissing her. "Jake—your sister. She must have thought me a complete loony. I don't think I said a full sentence to her any time we spoke."

He clasped her to his body. "Mmm...I love your nipples pressing against me. Shame on you...Mrs. Deerfield, darling."

Then his mouth closed over one nipple, the pulling and caressing sensation of his mouth tidal-waving the blood in her. When she thought he would lie with her, he kept her sitting on the side of the bed, bending his head over her legs, kissing her thighs, her knees, her ankles. Slowly his mouth retraced the route, until every bone in her skeleton had jelled and she could no longer sit without support.

"Jake, love me." The words pushed past her lips.

"I have since the moment I met you, and I have made love to you every second in my mind since then." He lifted her legs and swung them around so that she was lying supine. Then he leaned over her. "You have a perfect body and I love it, but I know now that it wouldn't matter to me if you had a leg or an arm missing." He looked at her as though each pore required scrutiny, then he lowered his body next to hers so that they were lying mouth to mouth. "I love you, Mrs. Deerfield." He touched her everywhere with his mouth, from her toes up to the tender skin behind her knees. "Darling, I love the scent here... what is it?"

"I can't remember," she breathed, taking air like a drowning person.

Jake's chuckle turned to growls as he intimately caressed her with his tongue.

"Jake, I have no bones. . . ."

"Darling, love, don't hurry it. . . ."

"Can't help it," she gulped, fastening her body to his and taking him into her as though she would imprison him.

"Siobhan... Vona... my own darling."

They spun away, planets and stars bursting around them, electricity creating a force field that none but they could cross.

Their bodies moist with love dew, they lay entwined, looking at one another, not able to control their love-drugged smiles.

"Making love in the daytime is nice," she giggled.

"Yes, it is, but it's dark now..." Jake's breath fanned her face.

"Is it? My goodness." Siobhan touched his cheekbones. "I'm very proud."

"Proud? Of what?" Jake asked, amused.

"Proud that my children will be so handsome, with dark, curling hair, and lovely cheekbones."

"My little girls will be tall and slender with red-blond hair."

"Are we fighting?" she drawled, hugging him tighter.

"I hope so. This is a wonderful way to fight."

"Yes, sweetheart." He nibbled the soft skin just above her nipples.

"Why did you give my...my diamonds to Andrew? Why didn't you give them to me yourself?"

Jake sighed, flipping her on her back and looking down at her. "I'm not sure I can explain that." He kissed one eyebrow. "I know how you feel about gift-giving, material things. You've mentioned more than once that you were brought up to value people, not things. I had the necklace made for you in New York, after you told me you were Vona Butler. I figured if you had something that belonged to me and my family, I could tie you to me even tighter." He stopped speaking to lean his forehead down on hers. "I have never been so insecure in my life as I have been with you." He gave her a lopsided smile. "Even now, in the newness of love, I have a doomsday feeling that you could be taken from me."

"Never."

He gazed at her for long moments, then continued, his voice hoarsening. "I can't describe what it was like seeing you for the first time in that diner. All the barriers and fences that I had so carefully constructed were kicked to pieces."

They watched each other, as though witnessing the crumbling of their personal fortresses, as though they were eager to see the people hidden so long behind the walls.

Jake's grin was slow in coming, but like sunlight hitting a stained glass window, it beamed over Siobhan in myriad colors, the spectrum striking her like a satin fist. "Mrs. Deerfield, I haven't made love to you in years. I'm hungry for you. Will you be my dinner?"

"Gladly." She pushed away his arms as they closed on

her once more, freeing herself so that she could sit up and stretch. Totally aware of his eyes on her body, she kept her hands high in the air and twisted left and right in sensuous movements.

"Vona, what are you doing?"

"Use your imagination, my sweet husband. I'm your Circe, your siren on the rocks." She moved her hands in sinuous invitation above her head, her body repeating the action, her eyes half-closed, but never leaving her husband's face. "I'm living out all my fantasies about you, my dreams. I would wake up in the morning crying because just as you were coming to me in my dream, I would waken. Then you were gone." She felt a strong heat growing in her body as she looked at Jake, who lay propped on one elbow, his eyes fixed on her. "I think I just became Mauna Loa, or Mount St. Helen's. . . ."

"I agree," Jake said thickly.

Jake's aroused body signaled his feelings to his wife. "Are you always going to tease me like this?"

"Don't you like it?"

"Oh, yes, I like it. In fact, what I think right now has been banned some places." The smile slid off his face, his eyes aflame.

Siobhan leaned over him and let two of her fingers trail down his body, trace around his navel, then drop lower, his rough breathing an erotic inducement to her. She pressed his arms back down to the bed when he reached for her, dropping lower so that she could sweep her breasts across his chest, her nipples tingling at the contact.

"Vona. . ." Jake's gem-bright eyes took on a glazed luster as he followed her movements.

Then he took hold of her hips and snuggled her tight to him, letting her slide down his body so that she became aware that her husband was fully aroused. His smile was a blast furnace firing her own passion. "Game's over, chameleon. Time to pay the penalty."

"So? What's keeping you?"

They made love in slow, rolling passion, Siobhan astride her man, delighting in all his love instruction.

TEN MONTHS later, almost to the marriage day, Siobhan had her baby at home in their Manhattan brownstone. There were a midwife and a doctor and one pale husband in attendance. Her labor was hard and long, but her strong constitution, buttressed by special food and vitamins and an exercise regimen supervised by Jake, took her through it.

The next day, as she nursed her daughter, Sara Jessamyn Deerfield, Siobhan thought she had fared better than her husband who sat on the bed and watched. "Darling, you need to get outside and get some color in your face," she offered, shifting her daughter to her other breast. "Oooh, one day old and she's pulling at me."

Jake's eyes, which had been riveted to the baby, shot to her face. "It hurts you? You should bottle-feed, then." His voice roughened with concern.

"You're still upset and worried. I can tell by your voice. It's all over, love." His wife reached out a hand to him, which he caught at once to his mouth.

She turned her head as the door opened, and the baby's nanny, Georgia Waters, came into the room, clucked over the baby, and lifted her.

"Mr. and Mrs. Deerfield are downstairs in the study. Shall I send them up? I've told them I would let them see Sara but that they would have to wear the masks and gowns I left on the hall table." Georgia, as she preferred to be called, pressed her lips tightly together and marched from the room, the baby cradled in her arms.

Siobhan stared at Jake open-mouthed. "She told your father that he would have to wear a mask and gown! He'll be furious."

Jake shrugged and moved to lie on the bed beside her. "You drove me crazy last night. I should have remembered how you cuddle in your sleep. I took two cold showers last night," he groaned.

Siobhan was still laughing when the bedroom door banged open. Jessamyn sailed in ahead of her husband, arms outstretched, her face wreathed in smiles.

"Darling Siobhan, she's beautiful, so perfect and so good. Jake had all that black hair when he was born. How clever of you to have a baby ten months after you married. I suppose you'll start a new craze." Jess barely inhaled. "People used to do things like that years ago when families were in fashion...but darling Siobhan, you're making it à la mode once more. Clever girl. Whatever made you think of it?"

Siobhan rolled her eyes at her chuckling husband.

"No doubt, she married a man who wouldn't leave her alone," David interjected.

"True," Jake concurred.

David leaned down to kiss Siobhan. "How's my favorite daughter-in-law?"

"Your only daughter-in-law, you pirate," Siobhan whispered as she hugged him. She had grown very close to her in-laws in the months of her marriage and loved to have them in her home or go to visit them in theirs. "How do you like Sara Jessamyn?"

"Well, I was going to send her back but the nurse said she just made the weight. So I guess we'll keep her."

Jess gasped. "David! Our baby!" She turned to glare

at her laughing son. "And don't you encourage him. . . ."

Siobhan grinned. "There's a bouillabaise tonight. Will you stay for dinner?"

"Yes." David didn't hesitate. "Will we be eating up here with you?"

"No, I'll carry her downstairs. She's getting a little cabin fever up here." Jake smiled at his wife, lifting his hand to her lips.

"Never mind, dear, in no time you'll be out on horseback again." Jess smiled at her. "Come David, I want to talk to the housekeeper about how to clean the baby's room." Jess kissed Siobhan and Jake then whirled from the room.

"She'll never accept that you're not an equestrienne in the champion class." David grinned at Siobhan. He kissed her, nodded to his son and followed his wife.

"Alone at last," Siobhan chuckled, watching her husband grimace.

"Don't remind me of my six weeks of abstinence, please."

"It will go quickly," Siobhan soothed, snuggling her head against his shoulder. Feeling desire move deep inside her, she admitted, "I may have to start taking cold showers myself." She turned her head so that they were almost face to face. "I never expected the happiness we've had—I never knew it could be like this."

"Have you been happy, wife of mine?"

"Yes, wonderfully so. You've made me a confident person—a calm, able, trusting individual." She sighed, searching for words to describe what the last ten months had been like. "I never considered marriage an adventure, but it is. I didn't know that the everyday details of living could be so exciting. . . ."

"Neither did I," Jake mused, making himself more comfortable on the bed as he held her close. "Challenge to me meant my business ventures, but the real challenge for greatness lies in our marriage—and our new family. That knocks me out just thinking about it."

"This chameleon will change no more," Siobhan yawned delicately, knowing she would nap soon and that her husband would hold her while she slept.

"Wrong, my love. You, my chameleon, have grown and changed every day and you will until you die." Jake looked down into her sleepy, love-filled eyes. "You see, there is no bottom or top to your love and your beauty, and each day it grows and changes, becomes richer and more of a delight. I love you, my chameleon, and I revel in all your changes—as long as you are here with me."

"And I love you, and I will never leave you." Siobhan closed her eyes, but even in sleep she felt his arms tighten, and she smiled.

THE AUTHOR

Danielle Paul (Helen Mittermeyer, Hayton Monteith, Ann Cristy) brings the theme of independence to many of her books. She was encouraged by her father to follow her own star, and has encouraged her four children to do the same. She married a man "so strong and gentle no woman could resist him." When Danielle isn't writing, she spends many hours working with the handicapped.